LIES ON ELMWOOD AVE

STEPHANIE SPEENEY

Honeyguide Publishing

ISBN: 979-8-9917488-0-3 (paperback)
ISBN: 979-8-9917488-2-7 (ebook)

To Ireland, the most courageously kind person I may ever know, my inspiration in writing and loving others fiercely and compassionately.

And to Rich, everything always.

CHAPTER 1

"Flight attendants prepare for landing."

The hum from the engine hardly drowned out the screeching toddler three rows up. *As if his anxiety and fear of flying weren't overstimulating enough.* He faced the window as the lights across Massachusetts shimmered like smoldering embers about to ignite from the sun soon to be set. Though it was mesmerizing, Ethan's eyes were vacant. The racing of his thoughts blocked anything from capturing his attention, disconnecting him from any semblance of awareness or appreciation.

Dread, it was dread that pulsated in his chest. White-knuckled, a rickety landing sends a rush of adrenaline through him. *On the bright side, if the plane goes down, I won't have to deal with this anymore.* Wishful thinking. Ethan looped a dark green backpack around his shoulders, pulled up his hood, and solemnly exited the gate.

Standing alone, among the bustle of arrivals, he located the black Escalade parked a few spots ahead of him.

"You Ethan?" gruffed the tan balding man in the front seat.

"Yep." With his left hand, he opened the door and skidded across the worn leather seats, hugging his backpack close to his torso.

"138 Elmwood Ave, Wellesley, right?"

"Yep." Ethan's hood sagged, landing around his ears.

"It's gonna take around fifty minutes. Traffic's a bitch. Here's a cord if you want to play music."

With a heavy slump against the corner of the door, Ethan's response was hardly audible and utterly false. "I'm good, thanks."

Ethan stole a glance at the GPS; four minutes until arrival. He took in the area surrounding his final destination: a neighborhood, quiet and, honestly, charming.

The car slowed to a crawl and he stepped out, his nervous system itching for signals to act on. Even the breeze seemed to halt while passing him, sensing the anticipation, as if to sneak by inconspicuously.

A two-story colonial, 138 Elmwood Avenue, sat back from the curb nearly twenty yards. Silhouetted by the evening light, aged pale blue shingles faded against deep navy shutters. The lawn was manicured enough to deny neglect but not enough to compete against the neighbors' meticulously placed daylilies, hydrangeas, and hostas.

Ethan turned, catching the red glare of the taillights retreating down the tree-lined road. As they faded, reality sank in. Ethan was alone, yet again, without a witness, to brave whoever was inside waiting for him.

Ethan smacked his knuckles against the wooden door. He hadn't meant for his hand to take the brunt of his anxiety, but he'd hoped the sensation would settle the shaking. The impact pushed the unlatched door open slightly.

"Hello?"

"In here!" a voice called from inside.

Ethan nudged the door open as far as he could from his side of the threshold, and then, he inched into the entry. The shuffle of his footprints echoed down the narrow hall, only to be drowned out by the intensity of his heart drumming against his ears.

The end of the hallway poured into a large open concept room. The kitchen was to his left, complete with an island that tucked it away from the entry hallway. A dining area with a large table filled the space to his right. Beyond that was a living area set in front of windows that spanned the back of the house. There lay two slender sofas parallel to each other, separated by a coffee table and accompanied by a chair to the left. To the right of this sitting area, on the far-right wall, was a floor-to-ceiling bookshelf

It was a man's voice that echoed across the space. Standing on the far side of the couches, his back was turned toward Ethan, focused out the window overlooking the backyard.

"Wild, right? I've never seen another like it."

In any other circumstance, Ethan would agree, but he was far too distracted to process his surroundings. The interior of the house was a stark contrast to the plain, traditional exterior. Mid-century modern furniture was placed throughout. Sleek, precise, 90-degree layouts, and yet also welcoming and warm. Not one detail or texture missing—it was complete. Even the throw blanket was folded in a perfect square draped over the center of the far couch.

What he could see of the backyard below would be better described as gardens. Assiduously planned beds with bright-colored flowers were situated among greenery, broccoli and kale plants. They seemed to lean in, to bask in the last sun rays of the day. Despite the structure and clean lines of the house, the gardens were *whimsical*.

Ethan's attention turned back to the man standing in front of him. He stood a few inches taller than his already lofty frame, dressed in a pressed button-down shirt and khakis. Dark peppery hair that matched his own was streaked with gray just above his ears. Admittedly, he wasn't who Ethan expected. But neither was any of this.

Ethan's hands went to the pocket of his hoodie and thumbed the paper inside, thoroughly softened from all the nervous fidgeting and sweat from his palms. He had received it just over two weeks ago. A plain white envelope with his name and address typed across the front. Inside was a matching card and a short ominous note. There was no return address or handwriting to identify the sender. But that context wasn't necessary to know what they were holding over him.

Ethan straightened his spine and cocked his shoulders back, attempting a threatening stance but his gangly limbs taunted him. The man was not so easily fooled, his additional 40 pounds gave him a clear physical advantage.

"Do you have it?" Ethan barked. More like yelped.

"Have what?" The man's response was smooth, innocent, curious, *infuriating.*

"You know."

The man continued his act with a hitch of his shoulders.

"What do you want from me?" At least this came out a bit stronger, Ethan's initial fear gaining an impatient edge.

"Kid, you don't know what you're talking about." Though blunt, the man's words weren't said to offend.

At this, Ethan tensed. "You sent me a letter." He shook as he took the crumpled paper from his hoodie pocket.

A smirk began to form on the man's lips, but his eyes remained kind. A sense of knowing spread behind them. "I did no such thing."

Ethan's irritation—no, eagerness for information—grew. A lengthy pause broke when the stranger reached into his pocket, and pulled out a nearly identical envelope, less crumpled and sliced with a letter opener, not ripped across the top like Ethan's.

"You're not the only one who got a letter."

Lightly placed footsteps sounded against the stairs, the pace painfully slow, like the maddening drip of a broken faucet. It started to make Ethan itchy. To his left, a small figure turned the corner of the stairs. Through the dimly lit living room, the details of a woman came into focus. Her deep hickory hair and soft features were aged into a frown despite not seeming much older than Ethan. Her frame was thin, like a piece of her could be snapped off with little pressure, but the look she gave Ethan suggested she'd bite anyone that got close enough to try.

The man spoke before she finished eyeing Ethan up and down. "Looks like we have company, Jade."

"Who's the kid?" The woman's head—Jade's head—nodded in Ethan's direction.

"Who are you?" Ethan blurted, indignant, and quite frankly confused.

She ignored the question. "Did you get a letter? Did yours have any instructions?"

"Instructions?"

"Hmm, you're not helpful. What did it say then?" Jade pressed.

"*Who are you?*" He was unsure who to face, he wanted answers from them both.

Jade cut in with a sharp retort, "Those details aren't important."

The man rolled his eyes. He unhooked his thumb from his pocket and extended his hand toward Ethan, who flinched, realizing too late the man was looking for a handshake.

"I'm Sam, this is Jade. She got a letter too." Ethan took Sam's hand and gave it a reluctant shake.

CHAPTER 2

Jade inched toward Ethan and brought with her a feeling of unease. A scent of lavender surrounded her like an aura, that, or a high voltage fence. Her tone softened, but in a way that felt like honey in a trap. "What was in your letter?"

Thankfully, Sam cut in before Ethan could respond. "Jade, if you won't share yours—"

"I told you." Her hand raised and head jerked toward Sam. "It had this address, a day and time to get here and said to wait for the rest to show up."

"And that's it?" His challenging words contradicted the gentleness of his voice.

"You know that's not it." She snapped.

Their bickering perplexed Ethan. These two knew each other and despite that, or perhaps because of it, appeared just as tense and defensive as he was. On top of that, she's horribly crotchety but this man takes it in stride. He shook himself from his observation. "Will one of you catch me up here, please?"

"Jade and I received letters as you did, with meeting details and a cryptic note. The lack of clarity is putting *some of us* on edge." The corner of Sam's mouth twitched upward as his thumb pointed in Jade's direction, somehow without her noticing. "And sharing your note might help shed some light."

Ethan calculated what was okay for him to disclose, "It just had this address, a date and time—8 pm." He played his best poker face.

"Just the address and arrival time? That's all it said?" Jade pressed, not bothering to hide her skepticism.

Ethan sure wasn't going to tell them anything. Not until he knew what the hell was going on.

Whether Sam accepted the lie or not, he didn't let on. "My letter is the same, but there's also a quote." Sam shuffled the cardstock out of its envelope and read:

> "Within the rows, those who look will find. What it holds remains hidden until held close. Only then can you embark, one at a time, discovering the secrets it was born to tell."

"What does that mean?" Ethan asked tentatively. Given what he was hiding, he didn't know if he was treading on sensitive ground.

Sam shrugged. "Your guess is as good as mine."

"What do we do now?"

"Nothing yet," Jade stated flatly. "My letter said there would be four of us."

Like clockwork, half an hour later, a rustling from the front porch caught their attention, muffled from the closed door. In unison, three heads turned sharply toward the sound. Heavy feet beat against the steps of the porch and softened as whoever they belonged to drew closer to the front door.

Ethan stole a glance at Jade, who had shifted her body behind a cabinet, hiding herself from view of the door. He snapped his attention to Sam who had removed his forearms from where they were resting on the kitchen island and crossed them along the front of his body. He leaned back against the countertop, positioning himself out of sight behind the corner of the hallway. Ethan took note of his own instinctual movements, slinking deeper into the room and shielding himself within the confines of the seating area. He crouched on the farthest seat of the couch, attention glued to the space where the fourth guest would appear.

The screech of rusted springs against their hinge announced the last to arrive at 138 Elmwood Avenue.

CHAPTER 3

"Hello?" The voice was masculine and sounded very confused. *He's not the only one.* "Anyone home?" The screen door eased shut.

"In here!" Sam called.

"Who the hell is that?!" Jade whispered with a snap.

Sam ignored her question, "No need for the language," he teased. That earned him quite the eye roll. Mischief flashed in his eyes as he continued. "The hell if I know." A small shrug, and a wink, "I guess we'll find out together."

Ethan stayed quiet, scrutinizing the exchange. If he'd known them for more than twenty minutes, he would have sworn a haunted expression flashed across Sam's face. Perhaps humor was his preferred defense mechanism.

A man stepped into view at the end of the hallway. Half bald, his remaining hair was a blend of gray and mousey brown. He wore thick-framed glasses, a hoodie, dad jeans, and those sneakers all the kids are wearing these days.

The new guy lifted his hand shyly in introduction. "I'm Robert. Ya'll got letters too?"

"Y'all?? Where did you come from?" Jade's nose turned up— apparently foreign to the concept of *Southern hospitality.* "Yes. We all got letters."

"Oh, I'm local, but I find certain vernacular charming." Robert donned an innocent smile.

"Ick," Jade whispered to no one in particular.

"I'm Sam." Right on cue, he extended a hand.

Ethan, eyes wide and brows high, lifted a hand from his place on the couch. An expression mirrored by Robert, a phantom recognition reflecting in his expression.

"This is Ethan and Ja—"

"Jade." She cut in, lips returning to their default frown.

Sam, Ethan, and Jade caught Robert up to speed. They shared their notes—well, nothing beyond what was previously disclosed.

Robert reached into his bag and pulled out his letter. It was crumpled and had a stain splotched across the back. "I have a code snippet in mine. It also has a unique signoff: 'Look for the signal'."

No one braved the interpretation of the computer code, they only paid mind to the end of the letter. An unsettling silence fell around them. *Look for the signal.* What was the signal? And what would happen *after* the signal?

Robert used the silence to catch up on his surroundings. He must have noticed the immaculate design as he fell into a trance while he took in the room. Dropping his bag, he wandered behind the couch where Ethan sat, making a sly attempt to catch his gaze as he passed. But it was unsuccessful; Ethan remained focused on his fingers, fidgeting in his lap. Robert's attention then locked in on the bookshelf which held countless hardbacks and trinkets. It wasn't what was on the shelves that captured Robert, but what was behind them. This particular bookshelf lacked a backing. It stood as a divider between this main room and a study beyond. Standing and stacked books blocked most of the visibility, but the negative space was enough to maintain openness between the two rooms.

He took note of the titles and authors that contributed to the shelf. "Impressive book collection."

Jade and Sam whispered around the kitchen island while Ethan studied Robert. Scanning the titles and sweeping his fingers over the tops of the books until he stopped abruptly among the G's. "Sam, what did your letter say again? The first line, the one with the rows?"

"Within the rows, those who look will find," Sam reread.

The corner of Robert's mouth crinkled upward forming a sly grin.

Sam asked what the rest were wondering. "Why?"

"Well, considering that, and the ending of mine…" *Look for the signal.* "…I'd venture a guess that this is where we should start to get some answers."

With that, he captured the undivided attention of the other three. Robert unshelved a thick midnight-colored hardback and held it up. On the cover was an illustration of a lighthouse whose light illuminated the title in dark text printed on the front, clear enough for Jade to make out across the room: *A Signal in the Shadows.*

CHAPTER 4

Jade and Sam joined the other two on the sofas and huddled around the book. Robert scrutinized the cover, the details of the illustration, the embossed inked title, and the copy printed on its back. Then he cracked open the spine. The air between them, already taut, began to congeal with suspense. With nothing but the sounds of aggressive paper flipping, Jade grew unsettled. Page after page. *What was he even looking for?*

The binding was notably creased down the center, halfway through the book. It caught her eye and refused to stop nagging her with every page turn. "Turn to the middle. Where the binding is bent to." Her voice was steady but her sporadic hand gestures gave away her adrenaline. Robert obeyed, letting the book naturally fall open to where it wanted.

A thin paper stuck out of the seam, the cluster of red font contrasted with the black text that filled the rest of the book. Robert plucked it from the binding and read aloud:

Sam, Ethan, Robert, and Jade,
Introductions should already have been made, but I'm sure one common denominator has been omitted. Each of you has a secret. Powerful secrets. The ones by which lives are changed, charges are

filed and millions of dollars are displaced. The consequences of which you all have avoided… up until now. Congratulations, I suppose, are in order. You have found my first, and arguably most uninteresting clue.

There are more of them for each of you to find. Successfully solve the subsequent ones and they will lead to a piece of incriminating evidence (your incriminating evidence). Find it before your past is exposed and you'll be able to leave here with your lives as they have been. Fail to do so and your secret will no longer be yours alone, the consequences of which will then lie in the hands of the three others you find yourself with this weekend.

Now that you are here, your secrets will keep you here. Should you try to leave before the weekend is over, the appropriate personnel will be notified, and you will be forced to accept the fate of their choosing.

Please be assured you are in no physical danger in this house. This act of retribution is not meant to be violent or dangerous.

Upstairs, there is one room for each of you in which you may stay, containing the comforts of your own home. *It might help to shed some light.*

Play nice and good luck.

Stealing glances at each other became a game as they passed around the book.

"This is ridiculous. Secrets? You guys aren't believing this, are you?" Jade stood and smoothed out the invisible creases in her pants. "This must be some sort of joke." Her body language and tone were consistent as she spoke, casual in a way that only Sam recognized as forced.

The collective silence was as good as a confession among the men, dissolving the deception she'd attempted with her denial. They had something to hide, and so did she, something that, given the inscription in the book, was bad enough to put at least one of them in jail.

"How do we know the threat is even real?" Her innocent façade slipped.

Sam was the one to respond, his tone teetering on grim. "Are you willing to take that risk?"

Jade's eyes flicked downward as she eased herself back onto the couch. The air around them became delicate. How fragile their secrets felt in the hands of these strangers. Was this for blackmail? A lesson? Punishment? The air thickened with guilt as they each considered their next move.

It was Sam who spoke again, addressing their small group. "Listen, I really don't care about anyone's *secret*, and I'd rather not know. Whoever this…person thinks they are…" he trailed off for a beat, "Obviously, we all have something we can't risk getting out. Can we all agree to search for these clues, not ask too many questions, and get out of here as quickly as we can?"

"Yes"

"Agreed."

"Yep."

Robert clasped his hands together. "Great. So where do we begin?".

CHAPTER 5

The four talked in circles, dissecting the verbiage of the letters and the message in the book.

Braving a potentially complicated answer, Sam directed a question toward Robert. "What function does the code in your letter serve?"

In response, Robert took out his letter and dropped it on the table with a spin. "It is just a fundamental snippet of HTML. This particular fragment is broken due to a missing character, but if corrected, its function is to anchor or hyperlink elements within the code."

Furrowed eyebrows and narrowed glances were exchanged between the other three. The drawing board seemed like a good place to go back to after that.

"There wasn't anything else in your letters?" Sam tip-toed on what he knew was delicate ground. From his tone, the others understood what he didn't say. *"You don't have to disclose anything, but it might help us get out of here quicker."*

Jade's head turned toward Ethan when his gaze fell.

With an exhale, his chin lifted, and he spoke. "Um, mine also had a name and date. And basically said that they have something of mine that I really need to get back."

This sparked some curiosity. *Something like a piece of*

incriminating evidence? Fortunately for Ethan, they didn't ask him to specify.

Sam raised an eyebrow "A name and a date? In addition to meeting details for this weekend?"

"Yeah, John, August 31."

"Does 'John, August 31' mean anything to you?" Sam asked.

Ethan shook his head. "Absolutely nothing. Do you think there's more to your letter? Maybe something else on the bookshelf?"

Sam considered the thought but didn't appear convinced.

"How did you find that book, Robert? That was awful quick." Jade's words dripped with suspicion.

Just like that, with one sentence, the room turned in on itself with a chill. This inkling of an accusation leaked enough doubt that they had to consider that, perhaps, they were not just four strangers with a common enemy.

If Robert was offended at what she insinuated, he didn't show it, but he did appear to be mulling over the doubt now brought to the surface as he responded. "Sam's clue, it's talking about a book. The message inside remains hidden until you…" He grabbed the book, now lying on the table in front of him, and with exaggerated motions, opened and held the book on his lap. "Only the readers, those who look, learn what the pages hold, one at a time." His fingers flipped one page and then another to reinforce his explanation.

"Plus, the shelf is alphabetized and that one was shelved out of order," he concluded.

Sam made his way over to the shelf and scrutinized the rest of its contents. Each remaining title was in alphabetical order. A dead end.

<h1 style="text-align:center">CHAPTER 6</h1>

Ideas came slower as eyelids began to feel heavier. Glances to phones and watches just confirmed what everyone was feeling; it was late. Given the high stakes, none of them wanted to end the night without a direction, but they had nothing else to go on. Each new thought was increasingly out there. Yawns filled long silences and tense bodies began to sink further into the couches. Finally, Sam suggested they call it a night.

Robert, Ethan, Sam, and Jade collected the items they brought with them and headed up the stairs. Even though their first clue assured them they weren't in any physical danger, it still felt safer to do things as a group. A very guarded and vigilant group, but together nonetheless.

The deep cherrywood staircase led to a long hallway with five closed doors.

"I did a little snooping when I first got here," Jade informed the rest. "These two doors are bedrooms and so are the two at the end of the hall." Her pointed hand flicked as she spoke. "The second door on the right is a bathroom."

Ethan stopped in front of the first door. Fighting against heavy eyelids, he was captivated by the crystal doorknob. Despite the lack of lighting in the hallway, there was a sense of illumination refracting from the swirled texture of the crystal. It shone against the wood behind it in soft, curved patterns. It wasn't just that the crystal seemingly glowed in the dark, it was that the concentration of light begged to be paid attention to.

Curiosity piqued, he took out his phone and flipped on the flashlight to play with the reflections. He knelt level with the doorknob and circled his flashlight around it, creating waves on the surface of the door.

The other three halted as well, watching his movements with differing levels of impatience. Robert seemed intrigued by the light refractions, whereas Sam appeared indifferent but that could have just been his tiredness. Jade's attitude was exactly as one would assume and just as obvious.

With the rotations, the shadows danced, etching shapes in the space just above the doorknob. The fluidity of the patterns enticed Jade and despite her impatience, she succumbed to its hypnosis. With a slight shift in angle, the design transformed, and then with a slight twist, they flowed into something else. Just enough for the new pattern to break her trance.

"Wait! Go back!" Tired and anxious were not her best look. Ethan's hand reversed in an attempt to replicate the previous position. The once wavy texture on the door formed into straighter lines and sharper angles. Letters appeared in an arch of concentrated light above the nob: Jade

"It might help to shed some light," Robert whispered, quoting the book's clue.

Sam half-exhaled, half-chuckled with a gentle clap on Jade's shoulder. "Well, looks like this is your stop."

Slack-jawed, Ethan shuffled to the room directly across the hall, circling the flashlight around the next doorknob. This time, it was his own name that flashed within the glow.

Robert wasn't content to let Ethan have all the fun. He walked over to the pair of doors at the end of the hall and leaned toward the one on the right. He replicated Ethan's movements, calling down the hall, "This one is mine!" when he finally found the sweet spot.

Sam walked to the last door. Standing in the threshold, he turned to face Robert, Jade, and Ethan standing in the doorways of their respective rooms. Stillness filled the hallway but a mutual tiredness softened the coldness between them. "See you all in the morning. Try to rest up, we'll need to be sharp to find the clues." With that, Sam turned the handle and slipped into the darkness of his room.

❧

Despite the hour, there was no way Jade was going to sleep.

Her room was as intricately decorated as the rest of the house. It was painted a pale yellow with off-white bedding and ivy green accents. A wrought iron bed frame matched the ornate curtain rod and bedside lamp. Resting beneath her feet was a taupe rug with a yellow and mauve floral pattern. She hated to admit it, but it felt so luxuriously plush between her toes she could melt. On the top of the dresser sat a plain jewelry box and alongside it, a glass vase full of yellow roses tangled among baby's breath and olive leaves.

At the recognition of the greenery, something snapped deep within her. *Olive leaves,* really? Her heart rate skyrocketed, and she ripped the covers away from where it was neatly tucked. Was this even real? Who gave *anyone* the right to mess with her life like this? She thrust a fist into an innocent bystanding pillow as she whirled.

She stomped toward the closet and threw the doors open. A dove gray robe hung from the rod. As she pulled it off the hanger her attention snagged on a very familiar tag. *"All the comforts of your own home."* She recalled from the first clue. How was this even possible?

She analyzed the rest of the closet. The top shelf was barren except for an additional pillow and a steamer. Sitting in the bottom left corner was extra bedding and a chunky knitted blanket.

She turned again, facing the room with stiff arms and clenched fists. Her glower went straight to the air vent in the far corner of the room, hidden almost entirely from sight by the puffy corner of the comforter and the dresser that stood before it.

"All the comforts of my own home, huh?" she gritted out

23

under her breath. She crept closer, peering down her nose into the cutouts of the metal grate. She knelt and firmly pushed on the right corner, and it sprang open with a pop. Carefully and quietly, she jimmied the cover, and it reluctantly came off, just like the one she had at home. She sucked in a breath as she reached in and picked up a black box. This, however, was not like home. Its cover was cool and smooth. With delicate fingers, she turned it over and, as she did, something shifted inside.

CHAPTER 7

Robert awoke the next morning to a loud thunk that shook his bed. You'd think the covers were on fire the way he tore them away as he sprang out from underneath them. He dressed quickly and snuck down the stairs to see what the commotion was about. Peering around the corner, he spotted Jade in a bathrobe layered over her clothes. She was clanking around, opening the cabinets, searching for something. On the kitchen island sat a black box.

She continued to open drawers and rummage through their contents, at last pulling out measuring spoons. "You going to just stand there and watch me or are you going to help me find the coffee grinder?" She didn't even pause to look in his general direction.

Now a light shade of crimson, Robert slipped in and knelt to open the cabinet closest to him. With delight, he lifted a small appliance and placed it on the island. Without thanks or recognition for finding it on the first try, Jade snatched it, repositioning it along the lengthy countertop next to the fridge.

"What's this?" Robert tapped the top of the box, yelling over the sound of coffee beans grinding. Once it stopped, she measured the proper ratio and placed the grounds in a filter in the top of the machine. The beep that followed might as well have been a cry of submission under the pressure of her slim finger and the coffee maker bubbled and burped to life.

"I found it in my room," Jade said over her shoulder. The flatness in her voice was either due to her extreme narcissism or desperation for caffeine but regardless, Robert couldn't take a hint.

"And you've stayed up all night trying to open it. Unsuccessfully, I reckon?" This earned him a silent glare, but at least this time she turned to acknowledge him. "You're still wearing yesterday's street clothes, and if you don't mind me saying, it looks like you haven't gotten much shut eye."

"You..." She swallowed her judgment of his quirky vocabulary. "...would be correct." She then turned and leaned her right hip against the island and held the box in both hands. "I've tried everything short of running over it with my car. It seems locked but there's no keyhole or hinge, for that matter."

"Mind if I take a look?" Robert offered.

"Knock yourself out." Her wrist flicked in his direction, holding it out for him.

Robert peeked up, slightly insulted because she made the retort seem equal parts literal and figurative. He reached for the box anyway. He analyzed the top, the sides, and then the bottom. "Did you see the inscription underneath?"

"The handwritten scribbles? Yes."

"...It's Japanese." Robert kept his eyes locked on the box, feeling the heat of embarrassment radiate off her as she neared to get a better view of the writing. "It says Karakuri. If memory serves, the term refers to a type of ancient Japanese craftsmanship, commonly where wooden figures are engineered to move using hidden gears and springs instead of electricity."

Jade looked up at him, confusion replacing her typical frown.

To that, Robert just shrugged. "In this context, I'd say it's a Japanese puzzle box or a Himitsu-bako. I did some work with a few executives from Japan in a previous life. Our client loved these things." He suppressed a shudder at the memory and continued, holding up the box and peering through his bifocals. "Typically, the exterior is more intricately decorated with wild patterns and such. It's obviously not authentic, but the mark could be indicative of how it opens."

The coffee machine beeped again, and Robert jumped, not from the sudden noise but Jade's jolt toward the empty mug she'd laid out on the counter. She leaned in as she poured, breathing in the aroma as it rose as if it would take her away from the present. Lifting the steaming cup, she took a long sip from hers and handed Robert a full mug of his own. He held in his shock and accepted it with a nod, interpreting this as her version of a peace offering.

After a few sips, a semblance of life returned to Jade's eyes. She crossed the room and took the end seat of the long dining table.

"Do I know you from somewhere?" Robert said, his finger on his lip, clearly trying to place her.

She didn't bother to look up from her mug. "You do not."

"Ya look quite familiar."

"Must just be one of those faces." So, the unpleasant demeanor wasn't actually caffeine related.

A voice echoed from the bottom of the stairs. "You wouldn't know her, she doesn't get out much." Sam appeared, having caught the gist of their conversation.

"Shut up, Sam," Jade sneered, but there was a soft edge to her retort.

"Trust me, you'd remember her. Hard to forget a grouch with that face," he said with a chuckle as he grabbed a mug from a cabinet and poured himself a cup. Despite the dig, her expression leaned more towards unamused than offended, her lips flicking upward with an eye roll.

"Creamer's in the fridge." Jade raised her hand in the general direction of the refrigerator.

Robert stood, silently surveying their interaction. "Y'all know each other, then?" It came out more of a question—he knew what happens when you make assumptions.

"Unfortunately." Sam and Jade both laughed, but the shadows remained in their stare.

"Care to share?"

"I used to work with Sam," she said, placing her mug onto the table with a lift of her chin.

"Not to split hairs but worked *for* me is a bit more accurate."

The corners of his mouth hitched upward as he spoke. At that, a familiar frown reappeared on the lady's face.

It was true, Jade did work for Sam. It was a temporary gig, admin work mostly, but it was an important stepping stone in forging a new career path.

Jade also knew Robert, and in fact, she met Ethan once but he wouldn't remember. Years before, in her 'previous life', as Robert would put it, she worked in a coffee shop most mornings and Thursday afternoons, the same one that both Sam and Robert would frequent but somehow never managed to cross paths.

Sam stopped in regularly on his way to work. 16oz mocha with skim milk. "I'm watching my figure," he would joke. He often chatted with her and the other baristas on shift. He complained about his long commute but that it was worth it for his kids to be in the better school district. Two kids, high achievers, but you could tell that was the expectation. Just like their father.

She was not surprised Robert didn't recognize her, but she remembered him. 20oz black coffee. He came in sporadically and only in the afternoons, often disheveled and on the phone. She knew he was some sort of nerd professionally but was never interested in details beyond that. To be fair, he didn't seem to care much about what she did either. It's not that he was rude, just always preoccupied. He probably had a lot to keep track of and didn't have capacity for much outside of that.

At this point in her life, Jade was miserable. Shocker, right? What was supposed to be a temporary job kept dragging out with no end in sight. She didn't feel stuck, because being stuck suggested there was a way out, and there was none in sight. That's why she was so grateful for Sam's connection helping her get to where she was now.

CHAPTER 8

Light slipped through a slivered gap in the dark gray curtains in Ethan's room. He woke up in the same position he'd finally fallen asleep in. For hours, he tossed and turned as images seared in his mind, as disorienting as headlights against the depth of night.

Ignoring the ache in his limbs, he used the crook of his elbow to block the light from his morning eyes. It felt like a dream. The letter. The clues. The book. Robert, Sam, Jade, and whatever her problem was. He pinched his eyes shut, as if it could shake him from this nightmare, then cracked open an eye from beneath his arm. It was no use; this was his reality for the foreseeable future.

The room was humble. The bed he lay sprawled in was situated in the corner on the wall with the door and opposing a single window overlooking the front of the house. Moody blue walls commiserated with the gloomy gray of the comforter. Solid colors and smooth textures made the room feel simple, not overly decorated but not neglected.

His eye caught on the nightstand next to him, more specifically, a small gold '68 Corvette toy car that sat on top of it. He'd noticed it last night on the shelf that floated above his bed. It was displayed among a small fleet of these cars, like a miniature auto show. Absent-mindedly, he ran his thumb over the side of the car, smooth and cool, unlocking a core memory from his childhood.

Ethan woke to a blinding stream of sunlight through the curtainless double window of his bedroom. The apartment was still. Tossing the covers away, he rolled until his legs fell to the side of the bed, and sprung up, feet sticking the landing.

A thwack of the door hitting the door stop prompted the padding of his bare feet across the hardwood of the hall to his mom's room. He shimmied through the gap in the door without so much as a squeak from the hinges. Taking three steps back for extra distance, he catapulted himself onto the queen bed, crashing into his mom who was still in a deep sleep.

She cracked one eye open and scooped him in closer to her, trying not to lose her sleepiness. Ethan inhaled her warmth but wasn't patient enough to snuggle for very long. It was Saturday, and it was time for test drives.

He and his mom spent the free time of their week building a web of racetracks for Saturday morning when they put their masterpiece to the test. A cobalt Camaro, a gold '68 Corvette, and a chunky blue rendition of The Mystery Machine flew through the air as tracks flexed or fell apart. The Camaro was his preferred test car, but his mom always chose the cartoon looking one. Said it was her favorite, though he never understood why since was the most top-heavy and flew off the track more often than not. Whenever it did, without fail, she would end up belly-laughing until her eyes welled up.

It was a warm sound, and sweet, like a hug but also like honey, just not sticky. It made you feel present, grounded, and overwhelmingly special.

For years they continued this tradition, even well into an age he'd be embarrassed to admit. Over time, his construction became sloppier, including sharper turns and steeper inclines. As he clicked the orange pieces together, he was no longer focused on exhilaration and speed while maintaining functionality, but on what configuration would make that boxy blue car fly the furthest.

A pang went through his chest as he placed the memory and memorabilia on the nightstand. Ethan tried not to think about his mom too much. It usually brought on a plethora of grief, loneliness, guilt and questions he would never learn the answers to but couldn't help wondering anyway. Why did it have to be her? Why did it have to happen to him? Did his dad know? Her loss was one mourned only on the surface; the counseling sessions hadn't felt thorough enough to reach the deep end of his grief.

Ethan knew better than to blame her for his spiral; that was his fault. But it did start when she died from cancer—malicious and undetected. Alcohol quickly became his coping mechanism of choice. At sixteen years old, it was a lot cooler than therapy and it involved a whole lot less feeling.

The bang of cabinet doors coming from the kitchen shot him back into reality. He pulled himself up, planting his feet on the floor and elbows on his knees. He rustled his fingers through his hair, palms attempting to wipe away evidence of a lack of sleep from under his eyes.

Ethan thumped down the stairs, a cup of coffee awaited him on the counter accompanied by cream and sugar containers.

CHAPTER 9

The four of them naturally spaced out around the living space. Ethan and Robert sat in the seating area silently eyeing each other over the remnants of their breakfast. Jade perched at the head of the dining table, her mug refilled. Sam leaned against the kitchen island, forearms cooling against its stone top.

"I'm startin' to get the feeling these clues weren't designed for us to solve individually," Robert said. The attentive silence from the other three encouraged him to continue. "The letters. The time of arrival and, therefore, order of arrival were planned deliberately. Finding the book was dependent on combining multiple clues. Jade found a clue this morning—a box. She didn't understand the inscription on it or its significance, but I did."

Jade's eyes shifted between Ethan and Sam, taking note of their reactions and feeling out the potential risk of everyone knowing about the box.

Robert continued. "What if we are meant to work together, at least for finding direction on some of the clues?"

Sam's head tilted back and forth. The theory made sense, at least given the few clues so far.

Ethan leaned forward, resting his elbows on his knees, resembling Sam's posture. "Why would we be forced to work together?"

"Torture, probably," Jade scoffed, her gaze hardly leaving the mug she lifted to her lips.

Robert shrugged in agreement. "At the very least, it makes protecting our pasts more difficult."

"And at most, it forces our hand to sharing them and puts us at risk of its consequences," Sam stated.

Robert brought the last sips of cold coffee to his mouth as he began more brainstorming. "Has anyone found any clues that could direct our next move?"

Shifting glances and sealed lips confirmed that yes, they did, and no, they were not willing to disclose whatever it was.

"Do you think there's anything in the garden or garage?" Ethan asked no one in particular.

"What about that back office?" Sam suggested. One head after another turned toward the study peeking through the slats of the bookshelf wall.

Ethan stood from his spot on the couch and followed Robert, who was already making his way over to inspect it. "Think there's something in there?"

"I'd love to find out," Robert replied.

Ethan, Sam, Robert, and Jade lined up along the bookshelf respectively, heads poking through the gaps of the shelves to better speculate what of theirs the room might hold.

Straight across from them was wall-to-wall shelving with cabinetry along the bottom half. Settled in front of that was a free-standing mahogany desk with a few ornamental accessories situated on top. Two matching wingback armchairs were placed to the left, in front of the windows that continued along the back of the house. In front of the chairs sat an oval coffee table with vertical wooden dowels lining the curved sides, creating a scalloped edge.

"How do you get in?" Jade mused.

Ethan poked his head out of line behind Sam and Robert, an eyebrow raised. "What do you mean?"

"There's no door," Jade stated plainly.

Ethan, Robert and Sam stepped back to inspect the shelf and then what they could see of the room beyond it. Jade was right, there was no doorway along the interior walls or cut into the bookshelf itself.

"Do you think we have to crawl through the shelves?" Ethan suggested, crouching in front of the lowest shelf, sizing it up next to Sam who frowned, hands resting on his stomach as if to say "*Yeah, fat chance.*"

Robert volunteered the next solution. "Perhaps we could climb in through the window."

They continued speculating, oblivious as Jade took a step closer and gazed along the seam where the inside of the bookshelf met the ceiling. Hidden in the corner was a track that continued along the wall of the dining area but blended seamlessly with the subtle pattern of the stamped ceiling tiles.

"Maybe there's a hidden door!" Ethan surmised.

"Think there's a removable panel built into the floor?!" Robert responded, wide-eyed in wonder.

Jade pinched the bridge of her nose as she listened to the increasingly ridiculous hypotheses. "While those are all *brilliant* suggestions…the bookshelf slides." She pointed a manicured nail toward the track. "The whole thing is the door."

They followed the line of her finger. Robert drew closer, removing his glasses for better scrutinizing. Sam and Ethan grabbed a shelf and started to push in the direction of the tracks. Robert followed suit and joined their attempts to slide the door open.

Jade paid them no mind and let her focus settle on a gold, coin sized oval stuck to the side of the bookshelf. Upon first glance, it looked to be a peephole, the top was flat with the exception of a little latch. Her fingers toggled the top. "You'd have better luck if you found the key first," Jade teased.

Their heads swiveled in her direction, skin warm and in various levels of disarray from trying to force the door open.

Her hand rested on her popped hip, the other propping her up against the wall next to the keyhole. It was written all over her— she was loving this.

Robert collected himself, retucking his now loosened shirt. He swung the top cover up and peered into the keyhole as if you could see through it. "I don't suppose any of y'all found a key in your room?"

Ethan went sheepish. "Um, no sorry. I didn't really look. I didn't realize we were supposed to look for stuff."

"Oh, I didn't do much looking either," Robert said, a bit too quickly, earning him a sly glance from Sam.

"Shall we go and look? Individually, I mean," Sam suggested, quickly adding the clarification knowing full well he wasn't letting any of them in his room.

"Might as well. We know we can't force our way in." Jade teased. With a shrug, they headed to their rooms.

CHAPTER 10

Alone again. At least this allowed her some time to think in peace. Jade untied her robe from around her and draped it over the ornate hook on the wall. Feeling the heat of mockery coming from the olive leaves across the room, she directed a vulgar gesture in its direction, hoping for the satisfaction of spite. The foliage lazily taunted her back. It was quite the touch. Whoever was behind all this went the extra mile for a guilt trip.

She froze at the creak of the floorboard and the squeal of a hinge behind her. Her head jerked to find a balding head poking through the doorway. She paled as she realized her finger was still pointed toward an inanimate object. Her arms recoiled, eventually leveling out into a fold across her torso. Her lips pursed, but it was the way her round eyes narrowed that made Robert nervous.

"Sorry, I should have knocked," Robert mumbled.

"Yes," she affirmed flatly. This brought embarrassment to Robert's face, still in the doorframe.

"Er, the box." His hand slipped through the gap in the door and pointed to the puzzle box sitting on the dresser. "I know how to open it. Well, in a general sense. Thought I could help if—if you'd like."

Jade was silent but offered a curt nod. She grabbed the box

and brought it over with her to the end of the bed.

Robert walked around to the other side, keeping his distance as much as he could to respect her personal space. He sat with one leg folded underneath him, the other foot planted on the floor. Tentatively, he took the box and placed it in his lap. His shoulders caved in as he turned it, familiarizing himself with each of its smooth sides and corners. He set the box down in between them.

He placed his thumb and index finger along one of the shorter edges of the top of the box. "There are slats along the exterior that, when pressure is applied just so,"—his fingers shifted, and a small horizontal strip slid three inches past the edge of the box—"will slide."

Jade's eyes tripled in size.

Robert continued, "There is an added layer of difficulty as it's painted black. The extendable pieces are harder to spot."

Her hand reached out to the opposite side of the box and mirrored the finger placement and pressure Robert demonstrated. A piece slid in the opposite direction, creating a symmetrical offshoot. She peered up at him, making an effort to soften the pride plastered on her face. He dipped his chin in acknowledgment as if to say 'impressive'. She dipped her chin back, 'thank you'.

"A specific placement of each of these slats will open the compartment inside. How you find that placement is with a code." Robert leaned his head over the box, angling his head to see through the stronger prescription of his glasses. In the dim light of the bedside lamp, he could make out small etchings on the unfinished wood that were previously concealed by the slat.

"Often boxes have inscribed symbols or numbers under the pieces. Like these, here." He nudged the box closer to her, his stubby nail pointing to the inscriptions. "When the slats are positioned to represent the code the storage compartment will open."

She leaned in. Carved in a line were a set of small numbers.

0　1　2　3　4　5　6　7　8　9

Jade snatched the box and put it in her lap, fingers flexing into a frenzy as she poked and prodded the remaining surface area on the box.

With as much self-control as he could muster, Robert watched, as if seated across from someone devouring their meal while waiting for the waiter to bring his own.

She eventually extended six more pieces, each with a set of etchings underneath. All of them were numbers, except for one which held a series of letters.

J F M A M J J A S O N D

"Okay, there are six sets of numbers, zero to nine, and one set of letters." Jade summarized, angling the box toward Robert.

"There are one, two, three, four… twelve letters in the set. But only eight are unique." Robert observed.

"It seems weird that there are repeat letters. If the passcode included a J, wouldn't there be three possible positions for the same code?"

"There would be." Robert paused to consider. "Unless, the order is significant, as in, they should be considered as a set. …"

Order matters, chronological. Twelve. Their gaze connected at the mutual realization. *January, February, March, April...*

"It's a date," they both whispered, a shadow of a smile reflecting off each other, however fleeting. Understanding fell upon Jade's face and Robert diverted his gaze from the box. The exhilaration of the puzzle was extinguished by a heavy dose of reality. He couldn't help but sneak a glance at the woman across from him. His heart plunged into his stomach when he noticed a faint scar that ran along her brow. Was the cause of that mark connected to whatever this box concealed?

Jade's mouth opened slowly but nothing came out. Robert's expression cut her off, hand signaling that no explanation was necessary. He rose from his side of the bed, leg unraveling from underneath him. With a small nod, he turned and slipped out of the door, granting Jade space to unlock the box, and whatever it held, in private.

With the quiet click of the doorknob, she was alone again,

but the room hadn't felt this claustrophobic just minutes before. Forcing her eyes from the door, she cradled the box in her lap. There was a date she could try. The mere possibility of it being the key made her gag. She tried, as she always did, to suppress the taste of ash that crept its way up her throat at the memory. The box heated, pulsating in her hands. She took a deep breath and pushed the pieces in place.

N   2   3   2   0   1   1

Nothing happened, no spring opening or indication that it had unlocked. She re-read the code, checking she adjusted the slats correctly. She had. Disoriented, she looked away for her eyes to rest, letting them go glassy on the vase of devastatingly beautiful yellow roses across the room. She didn't know whether to be relieved that wasn't the key, or... *but what if...* Her vision came into focus...on the olive leaves tangled among the flowers. She forced a dry swallow and began to shift the pieces to correspond to another date.

A   1   3   1   9   8   7

August 13, 1987. The birthdate of a woman named Olive James.

Jade's body throbbed. Her chest constricted, not allowing herself even the bare necessity of a full breath. With the last slat, there was a click, and the top half of the box separated with an easy pull.

Olive was a very plain girl, although she would describe herself as uninteresting or some other derogatory version of the word. Though meeting Olive wasn't unpleasant, it was just forgettable.

She felt like a fly on the wall of her own life, not truly experiencing it. Like it was happening to her, passive. She worked a dead-end job. She had few relationships in her life and the ones she had lacked rooting to feel truly connected. It made for a pretty miserable existence.

Olive found solace in long drives. She sat behind the wheel, listening to music to distract her from the noise of her own thoughts. In those sweet moments, she felt free. More accurately, it felt like she didn't exist anywhere, which wasn't altogether unfamiliar, but when she drove, she didn't feel the weight of living without purpose.

Despite feeling like her life didn't matter at all, she always went back home. Like a leash, she felt weightless until that jolting tug of the end of the line pulled her back in. She would always turn back around. And that truly drove her mad.

Late one particular evening she was out on a long drive after a closing shift. Winter was starting to settle in and she resonated with the darkness coming earlier and earlier each day.

Approaching that dreaded turning point in her drive, she pressed into the steering wheel with both fists, recklessly shutting her pooling eyes to will the tears to stop. She sucked in a choppy breath, letting her fingers ache as they twisted taut against the leather.

Taking the bend on Park Street too wide, opening her eyes too late, she couldn't react to the oncoming headlights. The impact shot through her. The scream of metal against metal was the last sound before the grit of smoke filled her lungs. Her car toppled and everything started to burn.

This was it.

This was how it ended.

This was how her miserable, meaningless, forgettable life would end.

Robert eased the door shut behind him. He paused, listening for movement in the rooms that held Ethan and Sam, and the one he just left Jade in. Satisfied with what he heard, he tiptoed toward the stairs. His sock-covered feet slipped across the living room floorboards, all the way to the sliding bookshelf. The fingers of his right hand swiveled the flap to expose the keyhole as his left hand reached into his pocket and took out a small key.

CHAPTER 11

Friday night, Robert entered his room feeling more alive than when he arrived. The book and the light-refracting doorknobs gave him a second wind. His mind was wired for games and puzzles. This one just came with the threat of losing his job, a lawsuit, and maybe even being ostracized in his profession, which only made it more riveting.

He stood just in the doorway and with an inhale, breathed in the details of the room. Immediately, he felt a tug from a computer on a desk in the far corner of the room. It was chunky, an older desktop model but not quite obsolete. His fingers itched to turn it on, but he let them tingle at his sides.

A warm glow came from a floor lamp in the corner next to the bed which was positioned along the wall to his left. Maroon walls blended into the black furniture and stood starkly against the red and gray flannel pattern of the comforter. Through the window directly across from him, he could make out the beds of the garden, coated in moonlight.

Three shelves floated along the wall on his right. These held a few small silver trinkets and a heavily used copy of *Coding for Dummies*. He let out a huff. What were they, trying to insult him?

Robert entered the professional world right out of college as a software developer, picking up jobs as they came in through various freelance websites. He quickly built his resume enough to gain a spot at a high-end coding contracting agency.

It would be thirty-five years this April, over the course of which numerous managerial promotions had been offered, which Robert had graciously declined—all except the first. Once promoted, his days were filled with boring meetings, follow-ups, and reviewing other people's work and lacked a hands-on aspect he hadn't realized he would miss so much.

People weren't his skill set, problem-solving and being immersed in the technical language were his skill set. Complicated, sure, but it was black and white. The code worked or it didn't, and if it didn't, you write a new function or find the missing character entity and then it worked. Yes, obviously, it's more frustrating than this implies but that was all part of his fun.

Robert negotiated a slight demotion and title change. His team was restructured so he still had a few direct reports and an intern but this hybrid role was more sleeves rolled up and in the trenches, as he preferred. He was back in his comfort zone.

Robert picked up the book from the shelf and fanned through the scuffed and stained pages. He had one just like it when he was in school; it had become a joke between him and his classmates. What started as a gag gift, actually proved helpful for quick reference in a number of his assignments. Holding the battered book in his hands brought him back, oh, the marks he'd accrued on his own copy. Coffee stains, salty snack crumbs, and the rough handling of college boys had left it seeing better days. In fact, one time it was returned to him by one of his cohorts with one of the pages ripped out! After that, he blamed any less-than-perfect scores on missing page 104 and swore to never lend a book to Billy ever again.

He was tempted to surrender fully into the bliss of reminiscing but the looming dark, albeit exhilarating, cloud of the weekend kept him in the present. The pages continued to whiz by, wafting a gentle breeze up to his face. With a skip, the book spread open, just under halfway. The next page, or what would have been, was torn from top to bottom, leaving little nubs of paper in jagged shapes lining the crease. Robert's tongue dried, feeling unnaturally thick in his mouth.

Page 104 was ripped out of this book. The copy in his hands was his.

Questions started to fizzle under his skin causing a shiver. How was it *here?* That couldn't be just a coincidence, could it? He hadn't touched it in years. God, what had he even done with it? He could have sworn he gave it to…the intern. He fought off the vertigo that accompanied the memories of the intern, the secret connected to the intern.

He started seeing spots. He shook his head, but the spots didn't clear. They were actually there, on the page. It was ink that bled through from the other side of the paper. He flipped the page. In thick black marker was a smudged phone number along with:

Text me what you see.

The gears in Robert's head shifted into deductive hyperdrive. Did this phone number belong to the one who organized the weekend? The area code was the same as his, so perhaps they were local? It was clearly intended for him to find. Would it be breaking the rules if he googled the number? "No, that's cheating," he mumbled, reprimanding himself.

Curiosity grated against him. What was he supposed to see? His gaze jostled around the room. "What do you see?" he asked himself. Nothing stood out. Perhaps he would have to hold onto this clue until another made it more clear. What would happen if he didn't wait? *What if he got it wrong?*

He clicked the digits into his phone. Once saved, he stuck the book in his computer bag deciding not to tell the others unless absolutely necessary.

Extremities tingling from the adrenaline, he turned and sat at the desk in front of the computer. He pressed the power button and the machine came to life with a hum and a slight rattle. His ears perked at the abnormal higher-pitched vibration. It was not in his best interest to have the others hear it and come check in on him. In an attempt to muffle the noise, he pushed his hand into the warm metal, but it only grew louder in response. Quick as a reflex, he jabbed at the power button, stopping the rattle and hum. Holding his breath, and every muscle of his body still, he listened for any movement outside his door. Mercifully, the hallway remained silent, and he took that as a green light to cautiously continue.

He reached for the computer tower, awkwardly lifting it to gain better access to the back panel. A clank came from inside. Yet another indication something was not as it should be.

Robert took a Swiss army knife out of his pocket, extended the closest thing to a screwdriver, and with the precision of a surgeon, started to loosen the screws holding the panel in place. With the last screw removed, he lifted the panel away, exposing the interior hardware of the machine.

Laying precariously inside the computer was a small key.

CHAPTER 12

Sam stepped through the threshold and eased the door shut when he entered his room late Friday night. He sat, gingerly laying his overnight duffle, a gift from his daughter, Lucy, on the bed next to him.

The blue and white striped quilt on the bed teetered on nautical next to the matching sun-bleached wood bedside table and dresser anchored in the corner of the room. Every detail was intentional, evidence of the time dedicated to setting the stage for the weekend.

Alone, he could now release himself from under the weight of his defense mechanisms: the buttoned-up front, the attempts at humor, the false nonchalance. He loosened the pin in this mask, letting the pressure dissipate, leaving his body limp, heavy, and downbeat. The sinking of his body into the mattress pad became a tangible parallel to the heaviness that filled his limbs. He'd spent his career in high-stress situations, mastering an unshakable poker face while under pressure. He never imagined needing to leverage those skills in a circumstance like this. Oh, how his life could fall apart after this weekend.

Absentmindedly, his toes anxiously dug into the shaggy, sand-colored rug. With a deep exhale, he closed his eyes, soaking in the calm before the storm.

Sam was a family man to his core, even considering his mistakes. He was married to Julianne for 32 years before she passed last June. Their pride and joy were their kids, Jack and Lucy. Both exceeded any expectations he'd had for them.

Still, Sam wasn't naive to the pressures he had applied nor the opportunities he aligned for them. Sacrifices had been made to give them the best future he could provide. He doubled his commute to move the family to an award-winning school district. No expense was spared for their success. Tutors, coaches, sport equipment, whatever it was, they got the best. It was a miracle they didn't rot one way or another. Before Jack was even born, Sam promised they would always be taken care of and would be after he wasn't around. The sizable wealth he had earned through the success of Summit Capital Group would be left to his daughter and son upon his passing.

Sam took after his father in more than a strikingly similar appearance. Both were wise, strong, and kind. Somehow, of all the things his dad passed down to him, his love for the sea felt the most potent. Sailing was a euphoric experience. One that couldn't be done justice when described, it had to be felt. The fire that roared inside his chest, and the lucidity that saturated his mind. That feeling bonded him and his dad, more so than the rest of their family. It was reliable, the way commanding a boat through roaring waters could revitalize the soul. Those early years, learning to trim the sails and balance the boat, made for their fondest memories together.

Well, with the exception of that very last time.

It was in this stillness that he noticed how quiet the house was. His home had become increasingly lifeless as Julianne had grown more and more ill. Just before the end, the radiance in her eyes had gone out, the one that would normally be sparked by painting with Lucy or feeling the crisp Massachusetts air.

Sam skimmed the rest of the room, his stare settling around the window. Suspended from the curtain rod by a dainty white cord was a windchime crafted from light driftwood and polished, brassy chimes. It was situated at the perfect height to be blown by the wind through an open window.

At the sight, the perpetual lump in his throat only grew more stubborn. He forced a sharp swallow and drew closer to it.

Odd by typical standards, for a windchime to be hung indoors, but it was not all that strange to Sam as he had grown accustomed to them placed this way. Julianne hung windchimes inside so she could enjoy them while she rested, dozing off to its soft lullaby as the wind wisped through the window. She'd often sneak the windows open, hoping Sam wouldn't notice the sudden chill that flooded the house.

Instinctively, he cracked the window, craving the comfort of the familiar crisp air and the delicate melody of the chime. As he did so, the wind rocked the curtains side to side, and he waited expectantly for the tiny symphony.

Its song was faint, practically nonexistent. Sam's fingers wrapped around the string, grazing the braided fibers as he delicately ran his hand down the length of it. There, at the string's end lay the reason for the stillness of the rods, the quietness of the chimes. The charm had been removed.

It was because of this silence that a new sound was able to steal his attention: a rattling. It slipped into the room through the space between the door and the floorboards. Sam crept over and cracked the door enough to catch the end of the noise, smothered quickly to an end. Closing the gap of his door to a sliver he listened, waiting patiently, expectantly, for any other sounds that may come from Robert's room.

CHAPTER 13

Robert's curiosity was killing him, standing next to the locked bookshelf. To be safe, he perked his ear once more in the direction of the stairs. All was quiet. He turned the key and loosened the door from its lock. Pocketing the key again, he tiptoed to the far side of the bookshelf. With a surprising amount of ease, he slid it a few feet creating a gap large enough to squeeze through.

Unleashed, he flew around the room with a stealth atypical for a man his age. His mind raced with possibilities. Was something held behind the art on the wall? Was there a hidden compartment nestled into the coffee table? Would a passageway open at the push of a button hidden among the books?

Slinking over to the mahogany desk, he eased open the top drawer. Laying on a stack of legal pads and yellow sticky notes was a flash drive. He straightened, going rigid. *"All this hullabaloo for a USB in a drawer? How utterly disappointing."* He swiped the flash drive and stored it alongside the key.

Just as he removed his hand from his pocket, a floorboard creaked. He gulped, realizing he may have just tiptoed his way into a hostile situation with one of his weekend companions.

Sam's figure appeared on the landing, frozen at the sight of Robert through the space in the open bookshelf. He paused with a kaleidoscopical expression, shifting between surprise and intrigue, betrayal, competition, and then truce. Robert's body tensed as he felt a rush he knew surged through both of them.

At once Sam was squeezing through the gap and into the study. As a team, they worked hastily and covertly, lifting book ends and paperweights and shifting paintings to the side, scrutinizing anything that could be a clue.

Robert went to the back bookshelf, skimming the titles and authors. He came across a thick photo album, one from the film camera era with clear plastic sleeves meant to store 4x6in photos. Nostalgia and intrigue drove him to lift the book from its spot on the shelf, resting it on the ledge of the built-in cabinetry that made up the lower half of the wall.

The first few sleeves' worth of pictures were blurry and grainy. You could tell the subject of each photo was the same small figure, but the angles made it impossible to make out distinguishable characteristics. He continued, the next set becoming clearer. The person was now bigger, older, and in the foreground of schools, sports facilities, and malls. In many photos, there was a woman who accompanied the small adolescent. Another page turned. The figure, male, now reaching adulthood, was captured nearly straight on, yet unaware of the photographer.

Robert's chest tightened, sending him choking on a staggered breath.

Already on edge, Sam rushed to Robert's side at the noise. It was not until he was within inches that he too recognized the quiet eyes and the deep, raven-colored hair.

Robert turned more pages, each was filled with candids of this man leaving work or the gym, in support group meetings, or out at restaurants. For pages, the collection spanned years of this individual's life.

The last page of the book contained only two photos. The first showed the man alone, looking washed away from the prior contents of empty glasses littering the bar top he rested his elbows on. More than half of the last photo was a blur of white, yellows and oranges. The overexposure created a silhouette of the man. His outline blazed sharply against the glow, perhaps a bonfire. He was slightly bent over, one arm extended like he was reaching for something on the ground.

The lump hardening again in his throat, Sam looked up at Robert. Sam shook his head and Robert understood: *This stays between us.*

But that didn't address the question that pulled the air taut between them. Why was there an album full of photos... all of Ethan?

CHAPTER 14

"Stupid ass key. How am I supposed to know where it is?" Grumbling, Ethan stood in the sunlight gleaming in through the window. He surveyed the room, unsure of where to even start. He was not cut out for stuff like this.

Feeling like an idiot, he knelt to search under the bed. Then he plodded over to the closet and gave it a once over. Next, he crept toward the dresser and pulled at each drawer. The first three were empty other than the rich smell of cedar. Holding his breath, he bent and opened the bottom drawer, which also was empty.

He wasn't expecting to find much. He was more of a 'hide in plain' sight kinda guy and when it came to seeking, his creativity was about the same. Aggravation took over and he flung himself, face first, onto the bed. With a thump and a clink, the headboard bounced up against the wall. Ethan's brows furrowed, brushing every different way against the pillow squished under his face. He lifted his head in curiosity, guessing there was more to that sound than the bed frame hitting drywall.

With a slight grin and a new sense of speculation, Ethan army-crawled to the head of the bed, shining his phone's flashlight in the crack between the mattress and the wall. An air vent tucked into the corner of the baseboard glowed in the light.

The leg of the bed frame must have knocked against it.

Ethan rolled, kneeled, and squeezed himself into the space between the floor and the bottom of the bed frame. Here, he was very glad Sam suggested looking individually because even with the circumstances of the weekend, he felt utterly ridiculous with his legs half poking out from the underside of the bed. With a shimmy, he directed his phone's flashlight toward the slits of the vent. Honestly, Ethan had never *looked* into a vent before, but what he found was more disappointment beneath the grate.

With more effort than he would like to admit, he freed himself from under the bed. Thoroughly over it, Ethan headed across the hall toward the room Jade had been staying in. Before his knuckles hit the door he paused to consider *"Is this intrusive?"* He knocked anyway.

A hesitant "Who is it?" came from inside the room.

"It's Ethan. Have you found anything?" The pause that followed made him doubt his whispering was loud enough to travel through the door.

"You can come in."

He inched the door open and peeked around it as if there were an armed bomb inside. That same scent filled his nose again, the one from when they first met. Jade was just sitting on the edge of the bed. Ethan's eyes flicked to the black box peeking out from behind her hip. He could see the unpainted interior compartment, confirming she had discovered something.

She tracked his glance and anticipating his curiosity, volunteered some select details. "I found this last night but just got it open." Ethan braved slow steps toward Jade and the box. He cycled through questions he craved the answers to but couldn't bring himself to ask. His inner conflict was palpable.

"No. It was empty," she said, reading his mind.

Ethan let go of a breath he didn't realize he was holding. A mix of disappointment and relief washed over him.

"I found something!" It was Robert's voice, muffled from traveling across the house. Jade and Ethan froze, locking bulging eyes. Ethan jolted toward the door and hurried down the stairs, allowing Jade enough time to slip something into the back pocket of her jeans.

CHAPTER 15

Robert and Sam stood expectantly in the sitting area, the bookshelf shut behind them, praying the glint in their eyes went undetected.

"I found a key!" Robert held it up, glance shifting from Ethan and Jade to Sam, effectively suppressing a knowing expression. They watched, captivated, as Robert inserted the small key into the lock, and turned it. The lock released a hiccup as it unlatched. Sam joined him and they both gripped a shelf, pushing it open as far as it would go.

Robert and Sam took the lead, looking behind the art on the walls and peering under decorations as if it was the first time they'd been in the room. Jade and Ethan followed, analyzing book titles and looking for signs of hidden compartments. Only the sound of clanking and clunking paperweights, bookends, drawers, and cabinet doors broke the tension.

"Interesting taste in artwork," Jade critiqued. Six trippy, bright-colored, abstract patterns were hung perfectly in line along the wall.

Ethan stole a glance at them before tucking his head into a cabinet. "Oh yeah, I loved those Magic Eye things as a kid."

In the corner of the room, hunched over a basket of what had previously been neatly folded blankets, Robert snapped upright.

He'd been so focused on looking behind the frames that he overlooked the art itself.

"Ethan, you're a genius!" Robert said as he crossed the room. Sam and Jade watched, missing the small twitch at the corners of Ethan's mouth.

Robert positioned himself a few feet from the last picture in the row. Brows scrunched, he gazed, but more like strained, at each frame. The look exchanged between Jade and Sam confirmed their mutual confusion.

"Could either of you please explain what's happening?" Jade asked.

The lack of abrasion in her request caught the others off guard. They passed around sly glances, each mutually delighted. Then Robert started this explanation.

"Magic Eye is an auto-stereogram." Blank stares prompted him to try again. "It's an optical illusion. When viewed correctly, there'll be a sense of depth within the pattern. There are often shapes that can look like three-dimensional cutouts within the image."

"They were big in the '90s," Ethan informed with a nod, evidently enjoying being on this side of a clue for once.

Squinting, swaying forward and back, Robert grew increasingly frustrated with the flatness he saw.

Jade lifted an eyebrow and glanced at Ethan, who was trying to hold in a chuckle. He was leaning up against the top of the cabinets. His shoulders curled in and arms crossed against his chest casually, back facing a space on the shelf that sat empty between two thick books. "Cross your eyes." He suggested with a slight shrug of his right shoulder. "That's the only way I was able to see it growing up."

After many failed attempts at crossing his eyes, Robert gave up trying. "Can you see it?"

"Well…yeah," Ethan admitted.

Robert gaped, "Why didn't you say anything?"

Ethan's shoulders flinched. "I didn't want to ruin it for you!"

Robert was flabbergasted at this waste of time while Sam's lips went taut in an attempt to suppress his entertainment. Even Jade appeared to be mildly amused.

"What's in the picture?" Robert asked, pinching the bridge of his nose.

"It's a letter actually, a W."

"And the others?" Jade mused.

Ethan lifted an arm and pointed from left to right, "J, I, G, S, A, W." *Jigsaw*.

Robert stiffened. *Text me what you see…* That had to be a reference to the optical illusion. Right? He suddenly became overly aware of his body, arms feeling unnatural at his sides and overthinking the bend in his leg. He tried to appear relaxed while shifting slightly from the others' line of sight and slipping his phone from his pocket. With trembling fingers, he typed a quick text.

Jade and Ethan began scanning the room for anything that could relate, even abstractly, to *jigsaw*. She opened her mouth, about to speak but was interrupted by a screech from the hinges of the screen door. Her head snapped and shot a panicked look at Sam who looked equally shaken. Four heavy thumps rattled against the front door followed by a deafening silence. Ethan jumped from his casual stance along the bookshelf, forearms clamped against his body. Robert blanched, both startled and guilty, assuming his text was what prompted this next shoe to fall. He prayed no one else noticed.

They tossed responsibility around like a hot potato. None of them dared move. Who was that? Was the person who organized the weekend *here?* At the front door? Did they want to be let in? Physical safety, shmysical safety, what if one of them got violent?

Sam's voice cracked. "I'll go." His shuffle echoed down the hallway and out of their view. "Hello?" He called.

There was no response.

A click and heavy pull of the front door shook the room. Stillness followed. Jade and Ethan shared a panicked glance, his face pale, her fingers pressed against her lips. Then, footsteps started again down the hall.

"It was just the UPS guy!" Sam called, his elevated pulse obvious in his tone. He reappeared around the corner, now holding a brown package.

"Don't come closer! Who knows what's in it!"

"It's not a bomb, Jade," Sam retorted, his words flat and laced with impatience.

"We don't know that!"

Sam rolled his eyes, stopping just outside the study, and shook the package in his hands. It rattled.

Jigsaw.

"It's a puzzle." Ethan was finally getting the hang of this.

Sam sliced the tape plastered along the edges with Robert's pocket tool and lifted the contents out of the package. It was indeed a puzzle. Its box, which would typically show what the completed puzzle would look like, was covered in thick, black paint—just like Jade's box.

They opted for the dining room table, dumping the contents out in a heap. Together they started flipping over the upside-down pieces and spread them out across the surface. In a frenzy, Robert started snapping shapes together. Ethan followed, unable to match his enthusiastic speed.

The colors consisted of complex blues and whites. Textures made of yellows and oranges contrasted with deep navy and azure.

Jade stood, less engaged with the puzzle and, oddly, more focused on Sam. Her eyes flared, willing him to look up at her, but Sam didn't sense her staring. He was zoned in on the pieces falling into place, wearing a stoic expression that contradicted the growing clamminess of his hands.

The blues were concentrated at the top with ivories that formed billowy clouds. The orange and yellow hues fit together toward the middle of the puzzle, creating a technicolor sunset.

"Is this a painting?" Ethan mused, holding a tile close to his face to take in the intentional brush strokes hidden in those details.

The top right corner came together next, and a long fabric sail started to take shape. Ethan and Robert were too involved in the puzzle to notice Sam's expression slowly change. Jade noticed though, and she continued her silent plea for him to look at her. Her lips formed a tight line, but he stayed locked in on the pieces coming together while water around the hull of a boat emerged.

Ethan placed a tile that completed the bottom part of the wheel and deck. Two pairs of legs depicted the passengers on the boat. One had longer khaki shorts on, presumably a male. The others' legs were bare, delicate, and feminine.

Jade caught the gleam of sweat starting to form above Sam's brow and upper lip. His expression now haunted, bordered on *dread*.

Piece by piece the scene came together, a radiant gleam of the sunset reflecting on the rippling waters behind the sail, brushwork blending seamlessly around the corners and in the details of the boat.

A moment in time, captured by this painting. It held a story, or a secret—one of a man and woman, gliding through endless silky waters, illuminated only by the lowered sun and the gleam of its brilliant hues scattered across the glassy sea.

Sam's heart thundered against his ribs. He held in a breath, desperate for some element of control, and waited for that moment. The moment the last free tile was placed into the puzzle. The moment Ethan and Robert stood back and took it in, looks of confusion coating their faces. Looking at each other and then at Jade and Sam.

The last puzzle piece, nearly centered in the landscape, the one that depicted the faces of the two people on the boat, was missing.

Sam's lungs released when he realized the piece was missing. True, he had accepted the fate of his secret coming out but that didn't make it any easier. He needed it to be handled delicately. He wished it was not with the four of them casually gathered around like this, solving a *blasted puzzle*.

His pulse spiked again when the others started looking for

the missing piece, searching under the table and on the chairs. Ethan and Sam retraced their steps, heading toward the back study, but Jade remained where she was.

Finally, Sam tore his stare from the puzzle and looked up at her. Her features twitched, lips pulling in tight, eyes blazing.

His brows came together, his head angling slightly. She sighed, and instead of rolling back, her eyes filled with pity. This only alarmed him more.

She slipped behind him and made her way to the study to join the other two. As she did, Sam felt something press against his back. Thin, stiff, and jagged. He reached an arm around to snatch away whatever she was holding against him.

His fingers wrapped around the small flat shape and with that, all color drained from his face. He let Jade reach the study before he did. Without so much of a hitch in his breath, he snuck the missing puzzle piece into his back pocket.

CHAPTER 16

Quiet fell over the house again as Sam, Jade, and Ethan gathered around the living space. It felt like hours ago that they'd assembled the puzzle, but then again, time hadn't passed normally since they'd arrived at Elmwood Ave. With no luck finding the missing piece, they collectively decided to take a breather and get something to eat. Though Sam's heart rate didn't fully settle, at least his stomach had returned from its visit to his throat.

Jade stood in the kitchen, brewing another pot of coffee. Her headache was probably stress-related, but she hoped self-medicating with another dose of caffeine would help. She peered up at Sam who was leaning up against the countertop. His arms were crossed in front of his chest and his focus thickly glazed over.

She'd feigned hunting with Ethan and Robert, wondering the whole time if Sam was going to say anything. Despite her curiosity, she stayed quiet, letting Sam control his destiny, at least as much as anyone could this weekend.

With a furrowed brow, Ethan took note of the absence in the room. "Where'd Robert go?"

Sam and Jade were too occupied with their thoughts to look up. "I'm not sure, the bathroom maybe?"

"He's been in there a while," Ethan said, sounding concerned at the possibility.

With the swing of a door, Robert's voice bellowed through the hall from the garage. "Hey, I found another thing!"

Jade turned to ice, numbness spreading down her limbs. Stiff fingers clung to the mug that became lead in her hands. Ethan, seated across the room, began coughing, trying to clear a dry swallow that had gotten caught in his throat. He looked up at Sam who was now a deep shade of cherry that splotched down to his neck and forearms. Their gaze crashed into each other and then darted to Jade, whose eyes flicked between them.

"But it's not mine." Robert came into sight and held up a round object, his demeanor falling as he read the room.

"Oh, my God." Jade wheezed a sharp inhale while Sam's shoulders released their tension. Thunderous heartbeats passed and then two brittle words broke the tension.

"It's mine."

It was Ethan.

"It's mine," Ethan whispered again.

"A hubcap?" Sam asked rhetorically.

"Wh—what's on it?!" Jade turned green, unable to look away from the crusted maroon stain smeared across and deep into the scratches of the plastic.

Ethan surged toward Robert and yanked it from his hands. He looked at it, blinking over and over and over again. Holding it sucked the strength from his knees. He pulled it into his chest, folding himself around it and collapsed to the ground, forcing raspy breaths into his lungs.

Sam, Jade, and Robert knelt around him. Their concern smothering the outpouring of questions about the hubcap and its backstory.

"Ethan, it's okay. Deep breaths." Robert murmured.

Jade flashed Sam a look.

Ethan's spiral continued inward and down. His fingers glowed white as he gripped the hubcap against him. His head was buried but the violent shaking of his shoulders told what was written on his face. He labored to slow his breathing, in his nose, out his mouth.

The hubcap, what it represented, snapped something inside him. For so long he had been hiding, lying. He couldn't do it anymore. The pent-up pressure was too much for him to contain. The truth needed to come out, and it came as if sprayed from a firehose. He began speaking, mumbling at first over his mangled breathing. As his breathing calmed, the words became coherent. No one dared interrupt as he told his story.

> Ethan had a drinking problem. It wasn't hard to admit, at this point he was over the denial stage. What had started as a way to cope with his mother's passing had turned into a full-blown addiction. He drank to drown his feelings, but the amount required to dilute them kept growing.
>
> One particularly lonely night, his birthday, he'd resolved to dampen his grief the way he typically did at a bar just outside of town. It hadn't helped, as usual, and the bartender cut him off, as usual. He didn't argue with the bartender, he just haphazardly pulled his keys from his pocket. Drunk driving was wrong, sure, but that doesn't cross your mind after quite a few too many, now does it?
>
> On his drive home, with his blood alcohol level steering the wheel, Ethan took a corner too tight. He couldn't see around the bend. Too inebriated to care, he ignored the warning of the oncoming headlights and failed to swerve out of the way. A collision, an explosion, but not his car. His vision went black, his brain barking orders to a puppet with cut strings. Through the shock, Ethan managed to shift into park. He fumbled out of the car, his pupils begrudgingly adjusting to the glow of the flames against the darkness of night.

The oncoming car had flipped from the impact, fusing itself against the guard rail. The side of it sunk heavily against the ground, melting, bitterly holding its driver hostage to burn with it. Bile rose to his throat.

Despite dulled inhibitions, Ethan's instinct was to help the passengers escape. He rushed toward the car, but then, he hesitated. What should he do? What could he do? The car was immersed in flames and his world wouldn't stop spinning.

Shattered glass surrounded the car like a moat. He stumbled with an arm reached out but an escaped ember singed his jacket and threatened to take him with it, so he drew back. Would he have been this cowardly if he had been sober? The thought made him sick. With the smoke he couldn't make out a driver or any passengers. Had there been anyone inside?

Returning to his car, he noticed his front bumper took the brunt of the collision. He inspected the damage, with the fire still ablaze warming his back. The wheels were fine, with the exception of his passenger front tire. The hubcap was missing.

Suddenly he sobered, or at least became clear-headed enough to know he needed to find that hubcap. It could prove his involvement; his fault. His gaze jolted. Where was it? Frantic, he spotted it mere inches from what was left of the flaming car's front bumper.

Reaching dangerously close to the flames, he picked up the hubcap. It seared through his numbed senses, but he forced himself to feel it. He raced back to his car and threw it on the floor of the passenger's side.

Shifting into drive, Ethan fled, tears painting stripes down his soot covered cheeks. His hands throbbed, and in response, he gripped the steering wheel harder. Drunk driving was already asking for substantial legal punishment, but killing a person?

Ethan would learn later that emergency personnel arrived at the scene not long after. The remains of the driver, a young woman, were not found in what was left of the charred car. She was declared missing, and after a short while, she was officially presumed dead. The perpetrator was not identified.

With no witnesses or evidence, Ethan managed to escape consequences; charges on account of motor vehicle homicide, and driving while intoxicated, at the very least. He'd gotten away with it. He would not be forced to physical confinement and marked with an official record affirming the title that tormented him, sunk its claws into him, ever since that night.

Murderer.

Jade was no longer green, she was ghostly. Sam's elbows pushed into his thighs as his fingers knotted in front of his lip. Robert remained still, observing Ethan as if the story he'd shared didn't entirely surprise him.

Ethan settled his shaking, his breathing slowly returning to a normal rhythm. "I need some air," He excused himself and slipped through the back door onto the deck that overlooked the yard.

With the click of the door, *it* got real. Whatever had just happened caused a shift. Before, it all felt like an escape room, just a game, as if the warned consequences wouldn't actually touch them. Despite the heavy pit in each of their stomachs and the shadows of their secrets, there was still a sliver of hope that this weekend, *the threat*, was not genuinely to be feared. That hope had been shredded to ribbons as Ethan's tears fell, his confession solidifying the danger still lingering for the rest of them.

"Well, shit," Robert finally said.

After a loaded pause, Sam stood and made for the back door. "I'm going to go check on him."

Jade lifted her head and glared at Robert, the unfortunate victim caught in her crosshairs. Before he could take cover, bile spewed from her mouth in the form of curses about Ethan and the type of person he is and where he should be. Her volume increased, emphasis sharpening, each time she mentioned *jail*.

"He's not a bad kid." Robert's tone defensive and matter-of-fact.

"Oh yeah, you and him go way back? Ever since yesterday?" Her typical sarcasm bore a new bite.

"Try to have some grace, Jade."

Jaw tight and teeth gritted, her fists grew white. "Some grace?! He hit someone while drunk and he *left*! He didn't even try to help that woman. He didn't care about her! The only thing on his mind was the goddamned hubcap that would prove it was him."

Robert gently shook his head, doing nothing to cool her simmering blood. "Are you so blinded by your own baggage?" She snarled back but he ignored her and continued. "That whole scene? That wasn't out of fear of being exposed, it was remorse. But I wouldn't say the same about you right now." He let his words soak in like oil into carpet. When he spoke again, his tone melted. "He's sober now, around five years, I'd guess, probably in a few months."

Without lifting her head, her eyes dialed in on Robert, now standing. "How do you know that?"

"He was in my Alcoholics Anonymous group years ago, before he relocated." With that Robert turned and headed for the stairs, leaving Jade to sit alone, to simmer with this new information.

> Ethan barely made it out of the shower before he collapsed. From fatigue, fear, and whisky.
>
> He woke the next afternoon, covered in sweat. Efforts to recall the details of the night prior were useless, the memories trapped behind a foggy

window. The pounding in his head reminded him why he was unable to remember the details. Had he dreamt it all? Like a cold plunge, the memory electrified him. The crash, the fire. The hubcap.

He sprang from his fog, ignoring aching limbs, and sprinted to the garage. His hands stung as he pulled at the passenger door handle, its hinges straining at the force of his throw.

It wasn't there.

Doubt spread through his veins like ink in water. The hubcap wasn't where he left it, or at least, where he thought he had. Didn't he grab the hubcap? How much of what he was able to remember was actually real?

CHAPTER 17

Ethan flung his backpack on the bed and began to shove the few belongings he brought with him inside.

He had the hubcap back. Its existence confirmed years' worth of nightmares and doubts. It was all real, he really was the monster he'd feared. And his secret was out. Sam, Robert, and Jade knew who he was, *what he was* and that he hadn't been punished for it. Rightfully so, they were disgusted, at least now he wasn't alone in that. They should call the police and leave him sentenced to the rest of his life rotting in jail.

His body moved without his command. Arms slumping his backpack onto his shoulder, legs carrying him, a deadened meatbag, down the stairs.

His trance was broken by a voice and it was only then that he realized he was only a few strides from the front door.

"What are you doing?!" Sam's words came out more forcefully than he'd intended.

Ethan was confused by the obvious question. "I'm leaving."

"You can't just leave," Sam said, his composed mask returning.

At this retort Jade's neck whipped toward Sam, the thin line of her lips not as sharp as the daggers that shot from her eyes, demanding him to *shut the hell up*. Knowing Ethan was still watching them, Sam risked a glance at Jade and sent her a pleading look. She knew what he couldn't ask for out loud. *A favor, after all I've done for you.*

"Why not?" Ethan asked, unaware of their unspoken exchange.

"The rules said we all had to stay all weekend," Robert jumped in.

"Or else what? You already know my secret." Ethan's tone hung between innocence and impatience. To that, no one seemed to have an answer.

"If you leave, the consequences are forced." Sam's words were solemn, humbly commanding the attention of not just Ethan, with whom he locked eyes as he continued, "but, if you stay, there's a chance… they may not be."

Ethan blinked. Robert's attention pivoted to Sam while Jade's fell to her hands, her lips sucked in between her teeth. Did he just insinuate he wouldn't spill Ethan's secret? Did this offer extend to Jade and Robert as well?

Ethan hadn't considered the possibility they wouldn't turn him in. He doubted Jade would pass up an opportunity to throw him to the wolves, she'd been visibly repulsed by the hubcap and his story. But perhaps if he stayed, and learned her secret, they could keep each other's.

"There's still the missing puzzle piece. Plus, we may need you for one of our clues," Robert said, layering on more reasons to stay. *And we can't forget about the creepy photo album.*

Ethan considered a moment. His answer came in the thud of his backpack against the chair. Relief passed through Sam and Robert, but it was Jade whose eyes burned.

"Robert, where did you find the hubcap?" It was Ethan's turn for deduction.

"There's a Camaro in the garage. That one's different than the others and appeared to be forced onto the front wheel."

A Camaro.

Robert didn't understand its relevance, Ethan did.

"God, I'm an IDIOT," he barked as he ran to the garage.

Jade followed swiftly after him. Robert started to do the same but a strong hand on his shoulder halted his momentum. Sam held him captive with a quick shake of his head.

By the time Jade got to the garage she found Ethan kneeling beside the front right tire. Tentatively, she stepped forward through the threshold. She watched him, zeroed in, examining the exposed metal of the wheel. Slowly, his fingers traced over the soot-covered rim. She could only observe, unable to will herself to move. Dust piled up and he switched to using the side of his fist. His pace quickened and she realized he'd found something under the grime.

Ethan looked up at Jade. "There's a riddle." And he read it aloud:

> Blooms of amethyst, a fine fragrance with a
> soothing touch. When tensions rise, I'm the
> one you clutch. Where am I?

With each word, the dark vignette around her vision grew wider. The air became too thick, suffocating. It wasn't that this riddle was meant for her, it was the message it contained: *I know more than your secret. I know you.* Whoever was behind this had been close enough to observe her habits and do so without raising any flags.

They knew that when her anxiety was at its peak, lavender oil was the only thing that seemed to help. That it became a security blanket, always keeping a roller applicator within arm's reach. And they knew she always stored a backup in her car.

Her eyes darted to the interior of the car. Scratchy words escaped through the tightness of her throat. "Look in the glove compartment".

Ethan's eyebrows knitted together but still obeyed. He hardly stood, more so diving through the passenger side door. Next to the handle of the glove compartment was a combination lock. One at a time, he rotated the dial to the code he didn't need a clue for. His birthday. The day he became more than a drunkard.

Vision still tunneled, she sensed the sliding gears under Ethan's fingertips. With each tick of the lock, a wave crashed into her. She was no longer in the garage on Elmwood Ave, she was tumbling in an endless, mossy, riptide. The chirp of the metal lock broke her vertigo, and forced her into the present, feeling like she had been drenched and drowned.

The cover hinged up. Inside was a faded newspaper clipping.

EXPLOSIVE HIT AND RUN: LOCAL WOMAN PRESUMED DEAD, PERPETRATOR UNKNOWN

Staring up in black and white was Olive James, the victim of Ethan's drunk hit and run, the woman whose life Ethan ended. Her headshot was paired next to a photo of her fractured and charred car. This was the first time he had allowed himself to look at her, to really memorize her face. He owed it to her after what he did to her. Hair described as strawberry blonde reflected as a soft gray in the newsprint. Her almond shaped eyes stared back at him. It was a shape he had seen before.

Ethan tore his focus from the paper and looked at Jade through the glass of the windshield, her expression unreadable. He slid off the seat and straightened, facing her from behind the open car door.

"Ethan," she whispered, like a hiker's attempt to avoid an attack in a wildlife encounter. "That clue wasn't yours."

He lifted his arm, the article still clutched in his hand and held it up next to her head just far enough out of her reach.

"Plea—" she started but the sound faded from her lips.

Ethan blinked. The almond shaped eyes of Olive James were the same ones currently boring into him with panic.

Olive James shot back into consciousness.

Heat seeped into her bones. Good Lord, it was hot. Plumes of smoke clouded her vision as did the dizziness of the impact. Mercifully, the shattered windshield allowed smoke to escape, granting her lungs small drafts of fresh night air. Alarms fired in every bend of her body. A slick trail of blood swelled along the side of her face. It felt cool against the heat billowing around her.

She hung suspended against the seat, caught in a tug of war between her seatbelt and gravity. Her hands, still clutching the steering wheel, were now covered in gashes, skin melting from the heat of the flames. She still had sensation in her feet, which was evident from the pain that shot through both legs as she attempted to move them.

She would be charred to death if she didn't get out now. Perhaps she was fine with that. She'd passed each minute of her life loathing her existence. Would anyone even notice if she was gone?

Held captive in this claustrophobic inferno, distinct from the injuries scattered along her body, an unfamiliar sensation pushed outward from the center of her ribcage. It grew, unwilling to be ignored. It was screaming at her: LIVE.

Life wasn't enough, she had that. She wanted passion, purpose, things so foreign her being ached to experience them. And apparently it took blunt force to the head for her to realize that.

Like the collision, it struck her—a plot twist of her own. A fresh start, a clean slate.

Staring down the fire consuming the car she was trapped in, she unclicked her seatbelt, strained against screaming muscles, and willed her legs to move.

This was how her meaningless life would end.

And it would be the beginning of her new one.

She laughed.

And then, she fled.

CHAPTER 18

Deafening silence smothered them.

"It was you." His words shrunk to less than a whisper as he forced them out. "You survived. I didn't kill..." A hand he swore was his eased the car door closed, removing the physical buffer Jade hadn't realized she'd been thankful for.

Lightheaded, Jade took a few steps back from Ethan. But he stepped forward, maintaining the proximity between them. Her mouth opened but no words came.

"I thought I was a murderer." His words were quiet but *electric*.

Her pulse spiked, adrenaline searching for signals to interpret.

The strength evaporated from his legs, and he braced his hand on the car's exterior for balance. Jade blinked and he was on the ground, palms fused to his lowered forehead. She froze at his movement, watching his chest rise and fall with regulating breaths. She inched closer and lower, mirroring his posture. Ethan lifted his head even with hers.

Her breath hitched. "You didn't kill anyone."

His hands reached forward, settling on either side of her face, and held it like she was just days old. She stiffened at the touch.

He didn't seem like the aggressive type but then again, she hadn't known him long enough to know for sure.

The warmth of his hands passed through the newspaper sandwiched against her cheek. With that, awareness radiated from his fingertips, and she understood what he was doing. He touched her like he didn't believe it was really her. He held her like an ornate, delicate vase, and he couldn't trust himself with fragile things. He stayed there, as if holding onto her meant she wouldn't vanish again. As if clinging to her equated clinging to the hope of what her life meant to him, what her life meant *about* him.

She let him feel the flushed skin of her cheek, to sense the rapid pulse beating underneath, allowing him to accept that she was here, alive.

It was this gentle touch that pressed into the wall she had constructed around herself. One that protected her from the things she refused to feel. Ethan's touch shook its foundation, forging cracks along its seams. It was the sight of wetness along Ethan's eyelashes that caused her own tears to fall.

Sitting across from Jade, his shoulders uncurled. Yes, he was still guilty. He chose to get behind the wheel of a car and drive intoxicated. He deserved consequences for his actions, and he would face them, for her. For the woman sitting in front of him.

The past she buried with the life of Olive James had been dug up. The story of her escaped death and true identity had a new confidant; coincidentally, the one to whom it mattered most.

There was an elation that came from sharing it with Ethan. A liberation she couldn't explain as she witnessed the look on his face when he realized Olive hadn't died. It was cathartic, intoxicating, redemptive.

This peace was short-lived. Her ribcage compressed, as if being vacuum sealed. She heard that inner voice again. *Tell him.* She ignored it. The truth he had accepted wasn't the full truth, but she couldn't face it herself let alone share it. It squeezed her again, this time in her gut. *TELL HIM.* She tried to push it down, but it erupted at her attempt. She needed to ease his burden as much as she needed release of the shackles her own secret still held her in.

With courage, she met his gaze once more. "It wasn't your fault."

Ethan's expression shifted to one of offense, responding to what he thought was mockery. She explained how she had recklessly taken that turn too wide, flirting with the risk of driving in the oncoming lane around a blind bend, eyes shut and teary.

His brows came together. He wasn't sure what to make of the ambiguity of Jade's involvement with the cause of the crash.

"No, I was—" His forceful words were cut off by her whisper.

"We are both to blame, Ethan".

He shook his head, but it slowed to a stop with her insistence. Silently, after long moments, their breathing aligned.

They didn't find Olive's remains, so she was marked missing only to be pronounced dead after little search effort. The whole car was incinerated for crying out loud. They could hardly identify the hood ornament. Without friends or family bothering them, the small-town police department was fine to close the case.

She miraculously made it out of the car with just the extent of some gnarly burns, sliced limbs from climbing out of the shattered windshield, and a deep gash along her brow bone. Against the ache of blistered skin, she fled.

Quick changes to her appearance were enough to ward off recognition. Her light strawberry locks were now painted a deep plummy brown. Makeup contours were easy enough to give an illusion of higher cheekbones, more arched eyebrows, and a stricter nose.

She got in touch with an acquaintance from her previous life, Sam, who was sympathetic enough to let her take on some administration tasks remotely at his company, connected enough to line her up with interviews, and gracious enough to not ask too many questions.

She later settled in New Jersey, accepting a job as an assistant, eventually working her way into roles she never dreamed she would be able to fill. And you know what, she was good at them. Really good.

This new life had purpose. In this new one, she felt indispensable, not so easily forgotten—even at the cost of niceties. Purpose, in Jade's terms, was finally within reach. Not without challenges, but a new motivation burned within her. She lived a life she hated, but that old her was dead. Plus, she'd always liked the name Jade.

Jade and Ethan sat knee to knee alongside the Camaro with tear-tightened cheeks.

Her voice cracked as she spoke. "I…" a swallow broke up her words. "Olive needs to stay dead." It was meant to come across more stern, but instead conveyed a question.

He had been watching his own fingers trace the edge of the article in his lap but, at her words, he looked up at her. Their connection was loaded; a plea, years of lies, hurt, and guilt. He muttered only one word in response. "Why?"

Her answer came as if she'd have no ability to stop once she started, keeping her voice low, only for the two of them to hear. "I can't go back to how it was before. This can't get out, I'll lose my jo…"

"No." Ethan cut her off, but there was no malice. "Why did you do it?"

Jade's eyebrows flicked together at the question, trying to find words to explain herself. "Olive…didn't have anything to live for. I didn't mean anything to anyone…I felt like I was wasting away a life I didn't even want to live— I… I saw a way out. Made an opportunity for myself." With those last words, she opened her eyes, starting to well again, as she relived the emotions she'd fought so hard to suppress. "But really, Ethan, you can't tell anyone, please. I'm begging yo—"

"Jade."

Her words caught at that name, the one she gave herself. She stilled, waiting for a sign of the fate she would need to prepare herself for.

"I'm not going to tell anyone." His hand, still clasped around the paper, lifted with intent toward her. Her lips formed a thin line as her glance shifted from Ethan to the article and back. She met his hand with hers and took the paper from his grasp.

He shuffled his leg out from underneath him and stood. Jade heard the gentle click of the door closing behind him and she took the deepest breath she'd managed in a while.

When Ethan returned to the kitchen it was empty. Sam and Robert had gone to their bedrooms for the night, perhaps to grant privacy to him and Jade. He yanked at the zipper of his backpack and pulled out the hubcap. He rotated it in his hands, this cheap piece of plastic he'd allowed to torment him.

His fingernail chipped away at the muck slashed across the front. Finding himself at the sink, he submerged it in a bath of warm water after coating the front in a thick layer of soap. He scrubbed at the stain, what he could only assume was evidence of Jade—Olive's DNA, and it slowly disintegrated into the water. His fingers caught on the scratches, like long scars, now visible that the blood had been wiped away. He rinsed the suds under the faucet and dried it with a cloth hanging on the oven handle.

Jade's footsteps whispered along the floorboards as she entered the living space. He turned around to face her, catching her glance at the clean hubcap in his hands. He hadn't noticed the depth of the circles under her eyes just moments before.

Ethan closed the distance between them. "I'll let you deal with this." He extended the hubcap, hands still pink from scrubbing.

Her focus teetered from the hubcap to the green and brown rings in Ethan's eyes. She swallowed the emotion that rose at the slight upward twitch of his lips. Instead of taking the hubcap Jade snuck her forearm under Ethan's outstretched arm and wrapped her other around his torso.

The gesture was certainly unexpected and *wildly awkward.* Despite the Jade he knew, it was gentle and genuine. He grinned to himself and returned it as best he could.

"I was so worried someone would recognize me when we first got here," Jade whispered into his shoulder.

Ethan paused. "Even if I had, I would have never taken myself seriously." He eased her out from his arms but held her where he could see the flickering in her eyes. "I swear I see…Olive, everywhere. Any woman could have been the one I killed. If it wasn't you, it would be another, it was only a matter of time. My conscience won't let that go." He felt her start to pull away and he gently resisted, keeping her within his reach.

"Ethan," her words bordering on melodic. "…you can let me go." She lifted the hubcap from Ethan's hand, freeing him of it.

Ethan's arms fell to his sides and he lowered his chin. He forced a deep inhale in through his nose and out his mouth, and then he let *Olive* go.

CHAPTER 19

Robert had been itching at any opportunity to get back to his room. Sitting in front of the chunky computer, he pressed the power button. It came to life with a quiet purr, the key no longer causing it to rattle. His left hand rested on the keyboard, as his right rotated the USB drive. It was basic and black, with no identifiable marks or indications as to what was on it. Robert plugged it into its port, fingers tapping nervously along the desk in anticipation for the File Explorer to load.

It held a single file. Unfortunately, a pop-up confirmed his assumption that this computer was not sophisticated enough to open it.

He scooched his chair out from under the desk, reassessing his options as he did. He could use his personal laptop, but doing so would obliterate an elementary rule in cybersecurity: Never plug in a flash drive from an unknown source. Who knew what could be on it? Malware, viruses? He twitched. *Who knew what could be on it? His secret? Incriminating evidence?*

The first clue promised he wasn't in danger, but did that extend to personal property? Could that even be trusted? He tensed, his expression curling from apprehension to regret. Security be damned, he needed to know what was on this drive. All his important data was secured, anyway. With a gulp, he thought of the cohorts that would gawk at this recklessness.

He pulled out his laptop and set it on top of his thighs. Muscle memory took over as he typed in his password and, habitually, placed his earbuds into his ears.

Am I really doing this? He was having second thoughts. Before he could talk himself out of it, he snatched the drive from the desk to smother its taunting. With a click, the cursor switched from arrow to rotating circle, and the file opened.

The screen went red. A vibrant red, as loud as the piercing alarm that blared through the headphones. He shuttered, nearly causing the computer to fall off his lap. With speed he'd never willed before, he flipped over the laptop and yanked the battery out before the third scream of the alarm. Tugging out his headphones he checked his surroundings. The house was still quiet.

Had it been meant to alert the others? Or perhaps it was just to rattle him. "Clever," He whispered with a nod.

His heart rate returned to its normal cadence and he decided to try it again. He kept the headphone cord plugged into the computer, but this time left the earpieces lying on the desk beside him. Again, the screen flashed red accompanied by the alarm, but this time, just a faint screech seeped out of the earbuds. It still caused him to shiver.

After eight long beats, the alarm stopped and the screen turned white.

CHAPTER 20

Sam sat awake, running his fingers along the curved and cornered edges of the puzzle piece—the act of mercy Jade had extended to him, however out of character it was. The way it played out was certainly not how he expected.

The featherweight brush strokes on the piece intricately depicted the shadows and textures of the woman's hair, and the gentleness of her eyes. Her beauty was painfully accurate, as if taken from one of Sam's own memories. She wore a man's button-down that grazed the top of her thighs. It blew softly in the same wind that tugged the sail.

The man had his midnight-colored hair in a style he hadn't worn for decades. His body was illustrated as it had been when he was younger, broadest from the shoulders down. A loose undershirt hung on his frame, covering the top of khaki shorts.

They looked at each other with undeniable infatuation. It brought back such gut-wrenching memories.

That last time he went sailing, he took a girl along with him, Marie. She had these mesmerizing eyes that you could stare at for hours trying to decide what color they contained more of. She was kind and gentle and not at all weak.

It was a stunningly calm night on the water, blissfully romantic too. Sam guided the boat toward the marina as the sun dipped below the silky waters. The elation of the night came to a stark halt with the recognition of a figure awaiting their arrival from the dock.

He secured the lines in a painful silence and helped Marie off the boat. He told her goodbye and Sam and his dad stood silently on the dock until her headlights disappeared behind the curve of the peninsula.

His father didn't yell, but Sam wanted to scream—anything to evoke a reaction other than the distraught disappointment written all over his dad's face. When he finally spoke, his words were hollow and, at the same time, made the air compress around them.

"Julianne called me at home. She asked if I knew where you were and if I could let you know she needed to take Lucy to urgent care." His gaze fell to the laces of his shoes. "She thinks it might be an ear infection."

Sam had never needed permission to take his father's boat out, but that night, it was clear a boundary had been crossed.

Sam never sailed again, never allowed himself to. It was too much of a reminder of his affair. It only felt right to withhold this joy as a form of self-inflicted punishment.

His father passed away unexpectedly not long after. Thankfully, it was peacefully in his sleep, but that didn't console the hole he left.

Sam watched idly as the boat was put up for sale and sold to an eager collector from the marina. His family was perplexed about the mask of indifference he wore as he handled the details of the sale.

What should have provided closure just felt like a

mockery. His love of sailing became permanently stained by that last time on the water. The lament in his father's eyes had seared into the last memories Sam had of him. Forever reminding him of what he did to Julianne, Lucy and Jack.

A torrent of emotions ripped through Sam. An echo of compassion for Marie, who hadn't known he was married. The tearing of his heart at what he did to betray his wife and his family.

In the moment, when he was young and ignorant, he blamed stress and overstimulation. He'd 'needed' an escape, to pretend to be a different person and avoid the details of his reality. His guilt told him he knew it would never be justification for what he did.

Owning up to it was long overdue. He owed the truth to his children, to Julianne, even though she would never witness his efforts toward making it right. He could never *truly* make it right but, God, he would try his best. Everything he did was for her, this weekend would be for her.

Sam wrung his fingers in his lap. He let these emotions encase his heart. It was less painful to be angry, even angry with himself, than to let his heart shatter from the sorrow of his own regret.

A familiar pain shot through his jaw reminding him to consciously pry space between his molars and he slipped the tile into a side pouch of his overnight bag. Then he opened the drawer of the bedside table. Illuminated in the soft glow of the lamp was a leather-bound book.

His head sank along with his heart. It would always remind him of Julianne and how he didn't deserve her or the unwavering love she gave him. She used to keep her bible, like this, in the drawer of the nightstand. He picked up the book and held it on his lap.

In the low lighting, Sam thumbed through chapters looking for a clue he knew would be there. He found it nearly three-quarters of the way through the book. The page was held with a vivid ornate floral bookmark.

This Bible was not a red-letter version, but the message stood out, coated in a trail of yellow highlighting:

> Then you will know the truth,
> and the truth will set you free.

This is it, Sam thought.

This was what Ethan had quoted from his letter. It was not a date or name, it was the reference. John, August 31 must really be *John 8:31*. This clue was designed to bring the two of them together, to push Sam into the tension of clutching onto his secret or sharing it with Ethan.

Sam shut the book, more forcefully than necessary, and flinched after in remorse. He lowered it back into the drawer exactly where it had been minutes prior like it had not been touched.

CHAPTER 21

Nothing. There was nothing in the file. No proof, no evidence. No direction. Just a white screen, as blank as his stare.

Robert recoiled as an image flashed onto the screen. Bizarre, especially in this context, it took him a few seconds to even compute what he was looking at. It was a fish, bug-eyed with a gaping mouth and a length full of shiny, bronze scales.

His head cocked to the side, his jaw jutting out with pursed lips. It wasn't a fish—well it was— but it wasn't *just* a fish.

The clue, the flash drive, the image, it was all a red herring. A fake out. He should have known that was too simple! How rusty he had become, able to be duped so easily.

Robert pocketed the drive and crept toward the door. He pressed on it firmly with his left hand as his white-knuckled right hand twisted the knob until it stopped. He eased it open enough to fit his ear through the gap. And then he waited until confident the others were asleep before he made his move. *He could do without a repeat of the bookshelf incident.*

That sweet, sweet silence gave him the go ahead to slip out further from his room, slink down the stairs, and prowl back to the study.

He paused a moment and took in the room now cast in shadows from the time of night. There wasn't much of the room they hadn't scrutinized already. While he had a new hunch to go off of, he decided to inspect other possibilities first: The area rug concealed nothing other than the same hardwood as the rest of the house, there was nothing sewn onto the backing underneath the armchairs and the coffee table was indeed solid throughout.

With those checked off, he circled back to the mahogany desk. He opened the top drawer, this time inspecting the detailing of the piece itself. He brushed his fingers along the sides and top of the drawer's interior. He did the same with the second and third drawers, giving a gentle tap to the underside, listening for inconsistencies in density, in case there was a false bottom.

He circled the desk, inspecting the side panels. In other circumstances, he would have stopped to admire the swirled and curved patterns carved into the wood. It was quite intricate, clearly high-quality craftsmanship, but those details were not important right now. He pushed and prodded at the curled shapes. They were all solid and stationary.

With more effort than he would admit, he moved the bulky wooden chair out from behind the desk. He patted the sweat off of his upper lip with a cloth from his back pocket and crouched down in the opening of the desk. Silky smooth wood made up the underside panels with a quarter-round border edge where each plane intersected. He swept fingertips across that connecting piece starting on the back left side of the desk and eventually working his way right, closer to the drawers. They rounded the top right side and continued on the edge closest to him—along the underside of the lip of the desk. The pads of his fingers tingled as they passed over a disruption in the smooth sanded wood. Robert gave a sly smile to the empty room.

He freed his phone from his back pocket, switching on the flashlight while he shimmied under the desk for a better look at the texture. Angled quite awkwardly on his back, he braced his body weight with one arm and held the flashlight with the other. There, carved into the wood, was an insignia. Three angles pointed upwards, the middle extending higher than the other two along with the letters SCG. To the untrained eye, one might think it the mark of the desk builder, but he knew better. He grazed his fingers over it once more, thumb resting longways over the letters. Mildly at first, he pressed in and the insignia lowered slightly into the wood. It caught, pushing back against Robert's hand and he responded with more force.

There was a pop and the squeak of a hinge. Robert flinched, squeezing his eyes shut. But when he opened them, nothing had moved.

He wiggled out from underneath the desk and checked inside the drawers. Everything was the same as it had been minutes before. He then circled the desk to inspect the front side. It was all perfectly intact.

Robert straightened to give his back some relief. Despite the darkness of the room and the prescription glasses he relied on, he was able to make out a tiny crack that now ran between the smooth top and the carved right side of the desk. He waved his arm with sass and a satisfied grin. "Ahh, a hidden compartment, that's much better," he sang to himself.

He slipped his fingertips inside the split seam and gently pried it open. The whole side panel moved, angling away from the desk. He speculated about the mechanics of the desk, about interior hinges that would allow the panel to swing down like this.

The gap opened larger as did Robert's gape. Nestled inside was a yellow document envelope. It was thick and bulged out at one end. Without a second beat, he snatched it, hugging it close to him. He knew what was inside without needing to open it. Proof. Evidence. Activity logs. A hard drive. And so much code. *His code.*

A grinchy smile spread across Robert's mouth. His free hand shot out with a flourish and gracefully closed the compartment. Light-footed, he pranced across the rug in the study, actually completing a full spin as he neared the sliding bookshelf. He sashayed through the living room and even continued his victory dance all the way up the stairs until he felt the hitch of the doorknob as he closed the bedroom door behind him.

CHAPTER 22

Sam woke up Sunday morning to the chatter of a bluejay teetering on a branch outside his window. The sifted light from the overcast clouds poured into the room, turning the pale walls more of a sad gray.

Sam sat upright, tugging his legs around so they hung off the side of the bed. Elbows laying heavily on his thighs, he rubbed stiff morning fingers against the creases in his forehead. With a long sigh, his head rose. This was going to suck, but it was time. He was ready for it, ready to embrace whatever consequences ransacked him today.

The staircase groaned, as did Sam, as he descended them. He turned the corner and greeted his weekend companions, already a third mug into their morning coffee.

Even in the cloud-stifled lighting, the dynamic between the other three was bright. Sam took note of the lucency of Jade and Ethan's eyes, like a clear sky after a storm, unwilling to be dulled by the shadows underneath. His heart ached at what he could only imagine they weathered together last night. However, tormenting, it was transformative, they seemed freed, more grounded, and more present. It was the most alive he had seen Jade. Ever.

Easy conversation filled the air between them, with genuine chuckles after one of Jade's well-timed sarcastic and undeniably funny jokes.

At first glance, Robert seemed over-caffeinated, but his hands and shoulders lacked the tense, jittery side effects. He was plain bubbly. Sam would have also noted the sly grin Robert attempted to hide if he weren't so focused on trying to appear as if he wasn't about to throw up, knowing that his biggest moral failure would be revealed within a matter of hours.

For what might have been a half hour Sam tried to muster the courage to speak. That first line he'd been rehearsing over and over in his head. He'd hype himself up to start in every lull in the conversation to be beaten to filling the silence, hesitating a second too long.

His hands were past clammy as the words came tumbling out over top of Jade, not registering that she was already speaking. "Ethan, your clue: John, August 31. I might have a hunch as to what it means." His words came out forced but Ethan and Robert didn't appear to notice. Jade did. Her brows rose and spine straightened, going uncharacteristically quiet. He held their attention as he continued. "Was it written: John 8:31?"

"Yeah, it was. Why, what do you think it means?" Ethan's question erred on nonchalant. His secret was out already, but he knew Sam wasn't in the same boat.

"I think it might be a reference—a biblical reference, as opposed to a date." He hoped Ethan wasn't embarrassed by his misunderstanding. Using that composed mask he'd perfected, he continued, "There was a bible in my room. I suspect that means we're meant to solve this one together?"

Still glued on Sam, Jade raised a brow with a lift of her chin. He met her gaze with a flash of an expression she understood to be a request for privacy, just Ethan and him. She responded with a slight dip of her chin.

The relief that washed over him was interrupted by the prick of someone watching him. Sam looked at Robert, who had caught his interaction with Jade. Robert's mouth slid to the side as he nodded as well, granting Sam his request, despite the tingling curiosity rippling under his skin.

✤

Sam sat on the bed in his room across from Ethan, who stood watching with his arms casually crossed across his chest.

"Are you religious?" Ethan inquired as Sam pulled the book out of the drawer.

"Not so much anymore, but my wife was."

Was. Ethan recognized the tone. He too was fluent in talking about loved ones who passed away.

Sam thumbed through the pages unnecessarily and eventually, the bookmarked page fell open. He explained the reference and how this was most likely what Ethan's letter hinted at. Ethan absorbed it with quiet nods and took the book from Sam when he offered it, continuing to flip through.

Sam's voice lowered to match the slip of thin pages turning. "I, uh, heard what you did for Jade, wiping the slate clean, I mean."

Ethan let off a little shrug as if it was no big deal. That, or he didn't really want to talk about it. Still, he responded, "Did you know about her?"

"She reached out after it happened and asked for help, though she didn't tell me many details. I didn't pry but tried to help where I could."

"You must have been close then, for her to reach out," Ethan stated, but it came out more like a question.

"Truthfully, no. I was taken aback when she contacted me."

"So why did you help her then?" Ethan asked with only curiosity in his tone.

Sam released a laugh caught within an exhale. "She reminded me a little of my daughter, who I've never been able to say no to."

Ethan didn't really respond, he just bobbed his head in acknowledgement.

97

"Why did you help Jade?" Sam asked.

It felt uncomfortable to be asked such an intimate question by a stranger. Ethan paused, at the boldness of the question but also in reflection, finally able to process his motivations. "Because I kinda get why she did it. She hated her life," *and I know the feeling*, "and she was so desperate for a change that she was willing to do…" he blinked, still astounded, "…anything, if it meant escaping that feeling." *She got a chance to erase her past.* "I mean, how often do you get a chance to start totally fresh," *without needing to trudge, fight, and grapple out of the hole you've dug yourself into?*

The tone, what he wasn't saying, was so raw it was palpable. Ethan's offenses couldn't be fixed with a new life. A fresh start would do nothing to remedy the past in the way he needed them to. It would do nothing to reverse the way he had turned to alcohol when his feelings suffocated him. It wouldn't change his actions the night of the accident, the damage he caused, regardless of the true outcome. It wouldn't alleviate the way his heart felt four times too big when he thought of his mom. And it would never loosen the vice grip of blame he placed on himself, for the father who refused to be in her life if it meant being in *his.*

Sam gulped, keeping his gaze on the book in Ethan's hands to avoid a vulnerable case of eye contact. He encouraged him to continue, allowing him silence to fill with his thoughts as he chose to.

"She's proud of her life now. If I took that away from her— even though I have my own thoughts about…everything…honestly, it would feel like killing her again." He shrugged, adding "You know?" to the end in an attempt to dissipate the seriousness. "Sorry, that was a lot. You didn't need to… never mind." He trailed off, becoming overly aware of how much of his heart had leaked out of his chest and onto his sleeve.

Ethan's words snagged on something deep in Sam and he lifted his head. In the same way, he could command attention in a corporate setting, he spoke, knowing he needed to hear it as much as Ethan. "I appreciate you sharing this with me. But

Ethan, you never need to apologize for your feelings. It is a lot, and it's important to feel them as they are. Having strong emotions is nothing to be ashamed of."

Ethan had been working on becoming okay with the sensitive side of him. For some reason, hearing it from Sam stuck in a way his own convincing hadn't been able to. Ethan gave a light-hearted shrug in response.

"You're very self-aware."

Ethan accepted the compliment, perking up slightly. "Thanks, my therapist would be proud." They shared a chuckle, but the flicker of sadness remained in their gaze. The last page floated by and Ethan closed the book and set it down on the bed next to Sam.

The rest of the room became more interesting as the space between them grew awkward. They began scanning the room as if scrutinizing for more clues but both of them knew they were filling the silence. Avoiding eye contact still, Ethan's attention landed on the bible that sat on the bed next to Sam.

The bookmark, still snug between pages, poked out a few inches from the top of the book. Vibrant hues of red burst against rich and earthy greens. Blooms and vines curled and wove their way from top to bottom. The bookmark, like the puzzle piece, was hand-painted. Sam's attention shifted to it as well.

"The bookmark." Ethan flicked his chin in the book's direction with a lift of an eyebrow.

Sam winced at the realization and solemnly, he said, "There are rose bushes out in the back garden."

Fireworks of colorful florals and barreling plumes of foliage filled the garden.

They walked through the rows of raised beds, scanning for anything out of the ordinary. In the back corner, Ethan noticed a hand trowel, neatly stuck handle-up in the soil, peeking through the leaves of a rose bush. He knelt along the front edge of the raised bed. Verdant branches spilled over the wooden borders, their thorns threatening Ethan as he grew closer.

Sam stepped alongside Ethan and they both began to dig. Labored breathing filled the air as they moved the soil around the stems of the bush. Ethan used the small shovel as Sam braved the dirt and roots with his bare hands, welcoming the way it stung and scraped against his skin.

The ping of metal on metal only fueled their adrenaline. Ethan threw the trowel aside and started to dig wildly with his hands, forearms burning as he did. A flat, emerald green piece of metal emerged through the loosened dirt.

Lying to rest in the earth was a tin box. Sam gripped the exposed end and pulled, but it wouldn't budge. They worked the soil loose around its edges, realizing the box was larger than they originally expected. Then Ethan tried. Grabbing the top of the box, with a hard tug he ripped it from the stubborn ground. It was refreshingly cool against his worn hands. The seal around the edges protected its contents from moisture and grime. A dirt-crusted clasp was all that held the box shut. All that held a secret from being released.

Sam stood and created distance between him and Ethan. When their gazes met, Sam nodded at Ethan, confirming he knew the box held proof of his secret. Ethan's mouth twisted and he offered Sam the tin with an extended arm.

It was the last chance to be the sole keeper of his secret. But he didn't accept. His hand lifted and shook, then rotated, directing Ethan to open it for him. Ethan's eyes widened, dropping his gaze to the box in his hands and frowned at it. He dusted off residual soil and placed his fingers around the latch.

Ethan would have seen Jade on the deck watching them with fingers pressing deep onto her top lip if it wasn't for the severity of the moment. Robert stood behind Jade mirroring the concern on her face.

From their vantage point, Jade could see what Ethan could not. The slow movement of Sam's arm toward the back of his khakis. From his pocket he retrieved a familiar square with oblong curves and sharp edges. The puzzle piece she had given him, the clue from her own puzzle box. The one that so skillfully illustrated Sam on the boat. The woman beside him a mystery to her, but obviously the heart of Sam's secret.

Ethan pinched the latch with dirt-stained fingernails. With a quick pop, the hinge flung open and sprung the seal of the lid.

Inside was a white envelope. Inscribed on the paper was, as typical, a name and address. It was stamped both with postage and the marks from transit. The handwriting was feminine, loopy, cursive, and italicized.

"Sam, this letter is for you." Ethan lifted his attention once more, hoping Sam would change his mind and take the letter so he wouldn't have to be involved.

Sam's bottom lip trembled but he nodded again, pushing Ethan to keep reading. Ethan settled the tin on the ground and, with dry dusty hands, unsleeved the paper from its envelope.

"Dear Sam…"

Ethan's eyes sped with ferocity as he read the letter's contents. Grappling for a voice to read it aloud but his ability to make even a sound failed. Sam's heart surged, his throat becoming like sandpaper.

Nearly ten years after his affair, the letter Ethan now held in his hands was delivered to Sam's work address. Along with it came a flood of guilt. Her, Marie's, writing mentioned a strong and compassionate boy, who had Sam's peppery hair. She wanted them to meet, for her son to meet his father and have a male role model as he navigated his teen years. The letter was a request, not a threat. His reply was immediate, firm and impassive, he would not consider it. He did, however, include funding for "support."

Months went by without any response. He wasn't expecting a rebuttal. Plus, the less communication the better. But, to his dismay, the pit in his stomach did not lessen. So, he sent another letter. No, he hadn't changed his mind, but this time the cash enclosed had doubled with the hopes it would alleviate some of his guilt.

Years went by and Sam sent more letters, each time the payout increased. Each time, the justification he told himself evolved. "What if this boy wanted to play a sport? He would need good equipment, and the activity fees were getting extra expensive these days," Sam reasoned. "He will need books and a computer for school. At the very least it could go toward his college fund. God, please have him go to a good university."

Still, no response came. As years passed Sam would calculate the boy's–his son's–age, what grade he was going into. Did he get his mother's eyes? Was he a good student? Did he have the hearty laugh he shared with his own father? Was he doing okay? Did he have everything he needed?

"...Love, Marie".

As he finished the last words, Ethan glared up at Sam.

CHAPTER 23

The once stoic man who stood so confidently was now blubbering before Ethan, as flushed as the roses beside him. Sam had one hand pressed up against the outpouring of tears, willing them to stop. His other hand stretched toward Ethan, holding something out for him to take. His shoulders convulsed and bottom lip seized as he shuffled forward a few feet.

Ethan took the object from Sam. The wheels in his mind mirrored the puzzle tile in his hands, rotating it around and around. The couple on the boat. The man, a spitting image of Sam, or what he would have looked like years before, maybe not that much older than Ethan was now. The woman, beaming at him, was illuminated by streaks of sunlight before their fate of setting below the horizon.

The warmth of their relationship, Sam and this woman, radiated out of the picture. The painter skilled enough to capture and evoke such emotion with mere brush strokes. Her arm delicately laid over Sam's shoulders as her head tilted towards his.

She was everything Ethan remembered. The angles of her eyebrows, which magnified the vibrancy of her every expression. Seeing her again ripped open wounds he thought had already healed over. He was caught, tugged between the sweet memory of her and this present torment. His stomach turned sour at the depiction of Sam so close to her. It felt too intimate to see her dressed only in a button-down, a man's button-down.

His mom.

His blood turned to ice.

Jade stood with her hand on her chest next to Robert who dawned a similar expression of mesmerized unease. The conversation below was inaudible from their vantage point of the deck, but the air buzzed with tension. Sam reached around to his other pocket and pulled out a handkerchief.

Occasionally, Ethan tilted his head down. Either to look at the clues in his hands or to hide his face, it wasn't clear. His grip locked around the letter and puzzle piece in each hand.

She felt wrong, like they shouldn't be watching such a private moment, but she couldn't pull herself away. Not even to steal a glimpse of Robert, equally paralyzed and hypnotized beside her.

Everything stilled, even the birds seemed to sense the tensions and refrained from their chirping. Ethan sat terrifyingly silent. His forehead, cast downward, was supported by his fingers as he gazed at his lap. Sam's tears slowed to a stop, finally able to catch his breath. He watched Ethan, the stillness starting to agitate his nerves. He had been like this for what was starting to feel like madness.

Ethan managed only a raspy whisper. "Did you know this whole time?

Sam trembled at the calmness in Ethan's voice. "The eyes, the, the brown and green… you have her eyes."

Ethan looked around for a place to throw up should the bile in his throat need to escape. First yesterday, now this? Why not just waterboard him with a firehose at this point? There were too many overwhelming things that demanded to be felt.

His mom. So tenderhearted, always his defender, and protector. Sam had used her, rejected her. He was helpless, unable to console her, like she had when he was young. And now here, she would not be able to comfort him like he so desperately craved.

His father.

His shock waned and he began to feel the pins and needles that filled his legs. Ethan rose from his kneeling position, lifting numb feet, one by one. Squaring up to his father, he peered down his nose at him with shoulders back. The fierceness in his eyes made Sam pause. His words did not fumble, they were assertive and fearless. "Your apologies and payouts don't put a dent in making up for what you did, how it hurt my mom and your family. This time I get to walk away and you're going to be the one wondering if I ever show up."

Ethan's steps barreled up the wooden staircase to the deck where Jade and Robert watched, eyes bugged out of their skulls, lips sucked in between their teeth. They stood paralyzed against the railing, gazes locked straight ahead on the foliage. Perhaps, they thought, if they stayed still enough, he wouldn't notice that they had witnessed the whole incident.

Heat radiated from him as he passed behind them. "What a f****** weekend."

If the crash of the back door against its frame wasn't enough to cause Jade and Robert to recoil, the surge it sent through the wooden panels of the deck would have.

Ethan and his backpack were long gone by the time Sam came back into the house. Jade and Robert had stayed, but only long enough to make sure that Sam wasn't going to have a heart attack and drop dead in the rose garden.

Jade left first with a nod to Sam communicating her thanks for his help along with her sympathy. Nothing was keeping her at Elmwood Ave. Ethan was gone, her secret safe in the hands that washed the hubcap clean. If Robert had more clues to find, she was sure he and Sam could figure them out without her. Plus, after the whole fiasco in the garden, she figured it would be best to give Sam some space.

She eased the door shut behind her and as she did, there was a tug in the center of her ribcage. It caught her off guard, the sensation a bit uncomfortable. It reminded her of a feeling she had at that pivotal time, one that urged her toward life. But this one was different, it wasn't restless, it felt more like…fullness. Like the space around her lungs had welled, but what had occupied the space wasn't heavy, it actually brought the opposite. She picked a piece of lint off her jacket sleeve and dismissed it, along with the feeling.

"Are you leaving as well?" Sam leaned heavily into his shoulders, palms braced against the countertop. His chin lifted from his chest.

Robert trotted across the living room with his messenger bag taut across his shoulder blades. With a nod, he held up the black USB, flashing Sam a mischievous grin over his shoulder.

At the sight, Sam's brows rose. Then a knowing smile grew across his lips stopping just below his weary eyes. He was glad for Robert, truly, as much as you can when you feel like your heart has splintered against the insides of your chest. At least one of them had gotten out of there relatively unscathed and secret intact.

Sam was left to pack alone. The house had become hollow, amplifying the noise of his movements. Even padded with socks his steps rumbled like thunder, the shriek from each doorknob piercing, the cabinets banging against their frame popped like fireworks.

He folded yesterday's shirt, then pants, and set them on the bed. Peeking out of his khakis was a folded piece of elegant stationery paper. One he'd received just over a year ago. The scent of his late wife swirled off the paper. He let it torment him with warmth and sorrow. Tenderly, he unfolded half, and then half again. He could recite these words from memory, having read them over and over and over. Savoring a few of her last words, despite the way they wrung his heart.

My dearest Sam,

I've fretted over telling you this for many years. It brings me no peace finally sharing it, but before I pass, I need to confess. I've known about Marie and the child. I found the letter she wrote you in the pocket of your blazer. Shortly after, I concluded the money that didn't align in our statements may be related.

I know you kept it hidden to protect us, our family, to protect me, and what this family means to me. But it was also an act of denial, of guilt for what you did—come on, you know I'm right.

Despite all of this, I need you to know that I forgive you and I love you. I loved you before Marie and I love you after. I love you despite the child and the bribery. None of this took away from what we had, although most days I wish it did. It kills me to say that I wouldn't have changed anything about how we pretended. Maybe it would have been better to confront you. But the risk of losing you, Jack, and Lucy was too much for me. I wanted our perfect family as much as you did. What really undid me was not the affair, it was that there is a child of yours in the world that is not mine as well.

It is because of this love that I am asking you to meet him. Please, at least consider it. Give him the chance to have a relationship with you. He deserves to know his father. He may reject you and, quite honestly, I wouldn't blame him, but if he's anything like you, he will come around *eventually*. He deserves more than guilt money, he deserves the privileges your other children have and will receive, including that of our legacy.

Promise me you'll think about it.

With all my love, Julianne

CHAPTER 24

Sam turned the lights off, one by one, while he wallowed through the house, his bag slung over his shoulder, keenly aware of the extra bulk from the photo album inside. Solemnly, he adjusted the bookshelf back into its original closed position.

He couldn't help the way his mind replayed the weekend. How it had devastated Jade and Ethan. The delicate strategizing they had to do to keep their pasts hidden from each other, those tortured conversations. The torment of reliving what may have been the most traumatic moments in their lives. His heart split further knowing the part he played in their pain.

His heavy steps carried him to the front door. Turning toward the living space from the end of the entryway, his hand held the light switch as he paused, facing the room.

There had to be a silver lining, he would tell himself, *wasn't there?* Despite the emotional torture, there had been a transformation. He had sensed it this morning. The renewal Ethan exuded, both rooted and featherweight, his shoulders no longer tensed in on themselves. Knowing Olive lived, knowing that despite his failure, he hadn't taken another's life. That she played a part in the collision and the disappearance. That the accident had spurred her to build a life she loved.

They had the release of a reset score. Receiving grace to resume your life, the worst of it out in the open, as if it didn't happen, and without the burden of concealing it with white knuckles any longer. Without it *holding onto you* with white knuckles any longer. Isn't that what he should be feeling too?

Weak fingers flicked at the switch and he waded through the shadows to the front door. In the yellow glow of the porch lights, he eased the screen door shut behind him.

The truth that came out about his own infidelity and relationship to Ethan, admittedly, could have gone better. But he couldn't say he regretted playing along and coming clean.

His stomach churned as he remembered the shock and betrayal on Ethan's face when he pieced it all together. When he had looked down at his mom painted on the puzzle piece and realized the truth—realized it straight in the gut. The anguish of it all ripping a new hole in an old wound. Knowing Sam had inflicted it all, then and there, and all those years prior. It twisted Sam beyond straightening.

He saw so much of himself in Ethan, *God help him.* Those words at the end. That strength! The empowerment, the confidence. Sam was proud of him. Was he even allowed to feel this way? As much as any absent father had the right to be proud of their child, he supposed.

Julianne was right, Ethan deserved to know who his dad was. Deserved to be able to choose to have him in his life or not.

Sam would come to accept it either way but hoped like hell Ethan could forgive him. Still, he understood the mélange of feelings Ethan was going through, and at least could try to sympathize. He acknowledged Ethan's resentment may never pass.

Sam turned, facing the navy door. He pulled his key ring out of his pocket, their jingle causing a lump to form in his stomach. He shoved the key into the lock, and spun it around until it clicked, sending a wave of nausea through him.

AFTERWARD

Tossing and turning, the night continued to slip away without rest as it had night after night. If Robert was honest with himself, he hadn't slept all that well since that weekend on Elmwood Ave. And if he was really honest, he hadn't slept well since he framed that girl either.

He'd effectively suppressed it before, so why was he unable to do so now? He had followed the instructions. Did everything he was told, and played the game, *and won*—if anyone was keeping score. That should be enough! And yet, self-reproach has ruined his sleep and also his sanity.

THE DAILY BOSTON

SOFTWARE DEVELOPER ADMITS INVOLVEMENT IN UNETHICAL PROJECT, FRAMES COLLEAGUE
Confession Unravels Scandal at Local Tech Firm

Boston, MA— In a shocking turn of events, Robert Hull, a software developer with a reputable history, has admitted involvement in a scandalous project from nearly three decades ago. Hull, who was tasked with building software for a client, recently revealed his participation in an assignment with massive ethical dilemmas.

The project in question raised concerns due to its consumer security threat and potential for misuse on a broader scale. The technology, upon completion, could be used to gain access into secured databases. On a larger scale, it could also be manipulated to breach major security protocols commonly used in securing confidential information from many well-known financial institutions.

Hull claimed he wrestled with the decision to build the technology but succumbed to heat from his employer. Remorseful, he deliberately added a hidden error to the code in the midnight hour before sending the final project to the client, ensuring the software would break upon deployment. However, Hull's attempt to rectify the situation took a dark turn when he decided to frame an unsuspecting colleague in another department for the error.

Additional sources revealed that Hull orchestrated the framing, planting false evidence that pointed towards a junior intern at the time, Julianne Patterson, as the one responsible for the faulty code. Julianne was immediately dismissed from her role.

Hull voluntarily turned himself into the company's management, confessing to his role in the scandal and revealing the details of the framing. This admission led to his immediate termination from the firm, most likely earning him a spot on the industry's blacklist. While the company decided not to press charges against Hull due to their oversight in the questionable nature of the assignment, the fallout has cast a shadow over the firm's reputation.

This situation has led to unintended and far-reaching effects and that's not even considering the substantial financial losses caused by the malfunctioning software at the time of deployment. Hull's confession led to a massive hit to reputations on both the client and agency side, resulting in severed ties after a long working relationship.

This setback became an unexpected opportunity for a rival startup to seize the gap in the market. The competitor's timely beginning and innovative approach resulted in a remarkable expansion, nearly tripling the size of the tech startup and resulted in massive gains for its investment group, Summit Capital Group.

As more details emerge, the case becomes more complex. Julianne Patterson, the framed intern, has been revealed as the late wife of Sam Patterson, the sitting Chief Investment Officer of Summit Capital Group. The coincidence has caused some to speculate whether more is at play but with such an expansive portfolio, no evidence can be found to support a connection.

This incident highlights the unpredictable and volatile nature of the tech industry, where the aftermath of one company's misfortune can pave the way for unexpected successes elsewhere. The scandal serves as a stark reminder of the importance of transparency, integrity and accountability in software development and beyond.

AUTHOR'S NOTE

Readers! I can't thank you enough for reading my book and for your time and support! It means the world to me! Sending you so much love and gratitude. What do you think? Do you want more?

Throughout this project, I had countless people tell me they *always wanted to write.* If this is you, let this be what you need to start writing, whether it be encouragement, motivation, or a friendly challenge. I could go on and on (I promise I won't) about the ways this book has changed me as a person and a creative.

Writing is a healer, it's a teacher, it's an art form. It *will* humble you, but it will also hook you. It's all part of the fun. And hey, we all start somewhere, am I right?

If you enjoyed it, (even just a little) and/or want to help support me as a new author, there are some things that would be *super* helpful and greatly appreciated! You could:

- Write a review on the platform you purchased the book (Amazon, for example) and on Goodreads, or other review platforms.
- Share the book with someone you think would like it.
- Share on social media and tag me! @stephspeeneywrites

ACKNOWLEDGMENTS

In the midst of corporate burnout, confusion, loss of direction and a lot of self-doubt, I set out in search of anything that would create energy. *To find a spark.* This book represents more than the countless hours spent writing its story. It's a challenge accepted. It's me against me, me alongside me, and me for me.

Though it was my special project, it wouldn't have been written, completed, or published (or possibly even readable) without the help of some pretty generous people. It's a huge honor to write their names in the pages of this book and to be able to introduce them to you.

Rob Bell, who I have never actually met, was pivotal in my decision to start writing and I feel it's only appropriate to thank him here. In his podcast, he offers listeners a glimpse of his journey writing a fiction novel, and let me tell you, listening to this, I sobbed. You can feel his exhilaration and I had never felt obsessed with creating anything like he had his book. It wasn't just a want, I *needed* that feeling, especially in the stage of life I was in. So, I searched for something I could spend hours on and not realize time had passed. Something I could use to inspire other creatives to do the thing that makes their heart sing. *Just like Rob.*

Rich, each and everything I create is for you and

because of you. Because of your encouragement to be brave, to be vulnerable, to be myself, to be the best me. Thank you for reading mere fragments when I was convinced the story was further along than it really was, especially since you will never willingly pick up a fiction book. Thank you for being excited for me, for cheering me on, and for not letting me belittle this project. Thank you for supporting our family in so many ways, allowing me the privilege to tell this story. It is an honor to go and grow on this adventure of life with you. *Love you to the 0% moon and back.*

Ireland Walton, who spent hours on Facetime with nothing but the sound of a keyboard clicking to fill the silence. For having so many words of praise and thanks for you, it's hard to find a place to start. You have opened my eyes to the world of this art form and kept me motivated. You are an inspiration, and you are my inspiration in much more than putting words down on a page. Your literary knowledge and skills are astounding to me. And the way you approach the world around you with curiosity, compassion, and conviction is something I look up to. The highlight of writing this was getting to do it with you, to share it with you, and to have an excuse to talk regularly. *Love you lots, Sis.*

Krysta Goldbach, affectionately known to me as "Baby K", thank you for being down to read this book in its early and quite unpolished stage. It's an honor of mine to have you involved in this project and to get your feedback on it! To share some of my favorite memories with you in college would be incredibly embarrassing (egg) but *I treasure them all (and you) so dearly.*

Jules Iepson, thank you for your generosity of your time, and your feedback on this story. Your perspective as a fellow mystery book lover was crucial in having this story become what it is. I kept imagining my book on your Instagram story one day and smiled knowing it would be extra special. *I hope you feel as proud as I am to have you involved in this project.*

Sue and Mark Walton, mom and dad, thank you for the unique gifts you passed down to me; My ability to articulate myself both effectively and creatively, my passion for creating, my diligence and drive, and my love for reading and storytelling came from the combination of you. Without those things, I wouldn't be the woman, wife, or writer I am today. *Thank you for that and so much more.*

Donna Speeney, thank you for calmly reading my book when I requested it in a panicked state and Kris Gibbs, your honest feedback was so greatly appreciated. It was an honor to have you both join in on my writing journey. Your high standards in literature was intimidating but made your feedback much more valuable. *Thank you both.*

Thank you to my editor Carol Trow, it felt destined to work with you. I hope you get to brag someday about how you were my first book editor. *Thank you for your help and support.*

Lastly, thank you to the friends who kept asking me "How is your book going?" and the ones I regularly forced updates on (sorry Taylor Dixon and Emily Tresca). You sensed this was a big part of my life and got excited with me, and I am so grateful for that acknowledgment, affirmation and company in it all. *Love you lots.*